GHOST
OF A
WHISPER

BETH DOLGNER

Ghost of a Whisper
Betty Boo, Ghost Hunter Book Two
© 2011 Beth Dolgner

ISBN-13: 978-0984915620

Published by Redglare Press
Book Covers By Melody
Print Formatting by The Madd Formatter

BethDolgner.com

For Karen Mosqueda

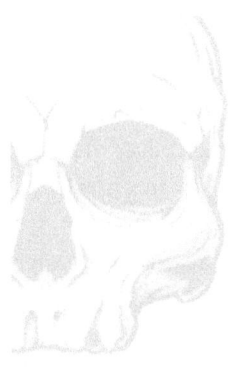

ONE

"You have to admit it's funny."

"And you have to admit that it's the best barbeque in Savannah."

I pointed at my half-devoured pulled pork sandwich. "You'll get no arguments from me on that point. But really, how did you ever decide to come to a place called Angel's?"

Maxwell shrugged. "A business associate suggested we have lunch here one day." He paused to delicately lick stray barbeque sauce off one finger. "I was hooked."

I giggled. The idea of my boyfriend—who just so happens to be a demon—eating at a place called Angel's was nearly as funny as the picture he currently presented. The sleeves of Maxwell's tailored button-down shirt were rolled up, and he was leaning forward over the table so as not to drop any sauce on himself or his dark gray slacks.

Maxwell looked up at me with his crystal blue eyes and gave me a wicked wink. "If I didn't know better, I'd think you were laughing at me."

I smiled in response. Maxwell and I had been dating for a couple of weeks now, and it was so far, so good. Well, after a bit of a rough start, during which I broke up with him, he saved my life, and a few people died.

Other than all of that, it had been going great. I hadn't

believed Maxwell was really a demon at first, but he had proved it on more than one occasion. He was responsible for two of those dead bodies.

I was responsible for the third. I was still coming to terms with that little tidbit. How did I, the perfectly normal Betty Boorman, wind up killing someone? Of course, I constantly reminded my conscience, it was either kill or be killed, and I'm just not ready to go yet. Especially when I finally had a boyfriend who, aside from being of the demonic persuasion, was a lot of fun, treated me well, and made me happy.

Finally, I put down my sandwich and wiped my hands with a paper towel. There were only a few other diners since it was six o'clock on a Monday evening. It was awfully early for dinner, but Maxwell was leaving town for a few days for work, so it was the best we could do. We were sitting at a rickety little table outside the old carriage house that the restaurant calls home, enjoying the late-September breeze.

"What are you going to get into while I'm gone?" Maxwell asked.

"I'll have plenty to keep me busy. We're getting phone calls and e-mails every day! Some of them are probably false alarms, others sound like people with mental issues, and a handful might actually be legitimate hauntings."

"Isn't that why Daisy volunteered to be case manager? To keep The Seekers from going on a wild goose chase every night?"

I nodded. "Yes, but it can be tough learning how to sort the urgent cases from the, well, the rest of them. I'm helping out as much as I can."

The Savannah Spirit Seekers consists of me, my best friend Daisy, her husband Shaun, and Lou, our all-around tech genius. The four of us go on paranormal investigations, something we started doing in college. We used to get requests to investigate maybe two or three times a month. Now we were getting that many requests in a day, and we were, frankly, overwhelmed.

I blamed Carter for our newfound fame. Carter Lansford might be my nemesis, but he was really talented at garnering publicity. When we had worked with his team, East Coast Paranormal Authorities, on a haunting at the Everett-Tattnall House earlier this month, Carter had managed to get us in front of the media. Twice.

As a result, I was now the latest local celebrity (though I was still nothing compared to Carter, who had a gaggle of fans and a book out), and The Seekers were almost as popular as Carter's team.

"I don't know how he does it," I said.

"Who?"

"Carter. How does he handle all this publicity? All these requests? I feel bad when we have to turn people down, but there's just nothing we can do about it. We can't handle every case."

"He's had years of practice at being the center of attention. Besides, it will calm down in a few weeks." Maxwell reached across the table and put his hand over mine. "I'm glad you've been so busy with the investigations, but I'm hoping you will keep the Saturday after next open for me."

I perked up. "Of course. What's going on then?"

"A Halloween party at Fort Pulaski. It's a little early in the month, but they didn't want to overlap with everything else going on in Savannah closer to the end of October."

Savannah, Georgia, does love Halloween. Considering it's the most haunted city in America, it makes perfect sense that its living residents would love the chance to do some haunting of their own once a year.

"It's going to be a formal event, so no costumes,"

Maxwell continued, "but I thought you'd enjoy being out at the fort at night."

I smiled. "It sounds fantastic. You know I'd love to go with you."

Maxwell made a face of mock relief. "Oh, good. I was worried you'd say no."

"But I will have to buy a dress. I don't have anything formal."

"Want me to come along? I can zip them up for you, then unzip them when you're ready to try on the next one."

"Something tells me I wouldn't get a lot accomplished with you helping me out of those dresses," I said.

"Probably not. It would probably wind up like Saturday night did, when I helped you unbutton your blouse, and your jeans…"

I could feel my cheeks blushing at the memory of our date Saturday night. Or, more specifically, the end of our date when Maxwell had brought me back to my apartment. Because he's a demon, Maxwell's temperature runs really high, so his skin is always warm to the touch. When it comes to any physical activity, he's positively burning up. What that means for me is that sex with Maxwell is different—and better—than anything I've known previously. Saturday night had been a perfect example of that, as he'd sent waves of heat coursing through my body with every movement he made.

I snapped out of my reverie to see Maxwell looking at his watch. He looked incredibly handsome, as usual. His pale skin, high cheekbones, and shock of black hair were a striking combination. He was tall and thin, and I admired how gracefully he moved.

"Time to go?" I asked.

Maxwell nodded. "I'm afraid so. I've got to get you home so I can make it to the airport on time."

I nodded, disappointed that our early date was already coming to a close. Maxwell didn't have to work a lot—he'd spent years building his business and now had the luxury of trusting other people to handle its day-to-day operations —but every now and then he had to conduct things himself.

We rose and began to walk. Since it was such a nice evening, we'd decided to walk from my apartment to the restaurant, even though it was on the opposite side of Savannah's historic district from where I lived. Maxwell took my hand as we strolled through the old streets and tree-shaded squares.

We were back at my apartment all too soon.

I opened the door and called inside. "Hi, Mina. Hello, Lieutenant Griffin."

Mina is my cat. Lieutenant Ambrose Griffin is my Spirit Sentry. The former Confederate soldier was killed at Fort Pulaski during the Civil War, and Maxell brought me his ghost as a gift. Lieutenant Griffin apparently has no desire to cross over, and he seemed happy to give up guard duty at the fort for guard duty at my apartment. I was still getting used to living with a ghost. He didn't do much— though he did like to bang on my window blinds—but I still wasn't quite comfortable with him. After all, he could be peeking in on me when I changed or took a shower. I hoped he had more respect than that, but ghosts tend to have the same personality traits in death as they did in life. For all I knew, Lieutenant Griffin had been a Peeping Tom in his living years.

In answer to my arrival, the blinds on my living room window swayed ever so slightly.

"I'm glad he's working out well," Maxwell said, following me inside.

"I haven't needed his protection yet. Let's hope it stays that way."

"Well, at any rate, I feel much better leaving you this week, knowing that he's keeping an eye on things." Maxwell turned to me and pulled me close, wrapping his arms around my waist. He leaned in and kissed me, the warmth of his lips sending chills down my spine.

"I'll miss you," I said.

"I'll miss you, too. I'm coming straight here when I get back on Saturday night."

I had already asked Maxwell why he couldn't just materialize in Washington, D.C., where he was going. I reasoned that it would be faster, cheaper, and a whole lot flashier of a way to travel. Maxwell had answered that, while he can materialize from place to place, his luggage cannot. Apparently it had taken him a couple hundred years to learn how to dematerialize without leaving his clothes behind. He told wild tales about scaring women during the Middle Ages when a naked demon suddenly appeared in front of them.

"Call me when you get in to D.C. tonight," I instructed. "I need to hear a voice that's not begging me to come investigate their loud plumbing or moaning air conditioner."

"I promise." Maxwell kissed me again and hugged me to him, running his hands through my short hair, which angled along my jawline. Then he kissed me on top of my head and disappeared.

It didn't take me long to wonder what I'd do with the rest of the evening. There were six messages on my answering machine: all people wanting The Seekers to come investigate their homes or businesses. One message was especially intriguing: a school bus driver wanted us to check out phantom wails and screams that she kept hearing, even when there were no kids on the bus. I put a star next to that one as I wrote down the messages. Even if it was just squeaky brakes or some other mechanical reason causing the noises, I figured we could at least be the first team in Savannah to investigate a bus. Even Carter's team had never done that.

It was the last message on my answering machine, though, that really got my attention.

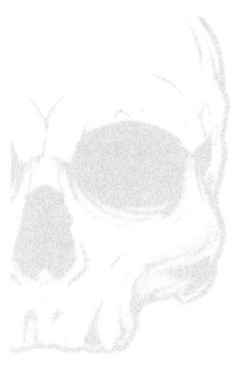

TWO

The voice on my answering machine identified itself as Azrael. Who would name their kid that? I wondered, but the next sentence answered my question: "Sorry, my name is Matt, Azrael is just my stage name."

Must be a hell of a show, I thought wryly.

Matt went on to explain that he was the organizer of Holy Terrors Haunted House, an annual haunted attraction. All I knew about them was that they helped the local food bank as part of their community outreach. Visitors got ticket discounts in exchange for donating canned goods. I remembered the house's advertising campaign from last Halloween, which read, "Bring food or be food!" The ads had pictured a zombie gnawing on a can of baked beans.

Holy Terrors Haunted House had, apparently, gotten some real haunts this year. Matt spoke of cast members getting scared during rehearsals because they felt like they were being watched and followed. He went on to say that things had gotten worse recently, with an apparently flirtatious ghost touching female cast members inappropriately.

I had to admit that I was interested. A haunted haunted house might even be more fun than a haunted school bus.

With that in mind, I called Daisy to give her the

rundown of messages. I was so relieved that she'd taken over as case manager. I get shy around strangers, but she was bubbly and outgoing, and she had no problem calling people back to discuss their situations in detail. We had agreed that she would never go alone to meet a potential client. Either myself, Lou, or Daisy's husband Shaun would go along.

Daisy was as excited about the haunted house as I was, but for a totally different reason. "I love haunted houses!" She said it so loudly that I actually had to hold the phone away from my ear. "It would be way cool to go in and see a haunt with all the lights on and to see behind the scenes."

"Wouldn't that kind of ruin the illusion for you?"

"No way. It would make me appreciate the place even more. We could investigate, then go back one night and get good and scared."

"I'll be happy to scream my head off with you," I promised. I was a fan of haunted houses, too, and Daisy and I could both scream with the best of them. I figured it was good for us: we got it out of our systems so we wouldn't scream if something strange happened on a real investigation.

We said our good-byes and hung up, so I was pretty surprised when my phone rang again just ten minutes later, and I heard Daisy's voice again.

"Can you go with me to meet this Matt character? He says he has tomorrow night open."

"That was fast. Sure. I can pick you up. What time?"

"Seven."

Daisy was so excited that I could practically see her grinning through the phone. Even if we showed up at the meeting and debunked the paranormal claims in the first five minutes, I suspected she might still accept the case just for the chance to see the inner workings of the haunted house.

Work rushed by on Tuesday. Ever since my boss at Coastal Health Hospital had suggested that my ghost hunting interfered with my work as a marketing assistant, I had been on my best behavior. And, I figured, the best way to stay on task was to stay busy. I found myself volunteering to take on all kinds of extra work. It made my workload heavier but, on the upside, it meant my days passed really quickly.

I didn't want to show up at the haunted house in my work clothes, so after I got home, I changed into jeans and my black Savannah Spirit Seekers tee-shirt. We had gotten them made to celebrate our success at the Everett-Tattnall House. Our name was written in red and white script across the left breast, and the back featured a logo that Shaun had designed for us, with a cartoon ghost forming the "S" in "Spirit."

Maxwell called me on my drive to Daisy's house, and it sounded like his day had been even busier than mine. I missed him already, and he'd only been gone one night.

We wrapped up our conversation just as I pulled into Daisy and Shaun's driveway. They live in an older suburb just outside the historic district, where I live. Their ranch-style house is a lot roomier than my little apartment on the bottom floor of an old carriage house. I had once told Daisy that my place had plenty of character, which was about all I could fit in the tiny space.

Daisy answered the door in her Seekers tee, so we made a matching pair. It was odd to see her in black, though. Daisy has blonde curls and usually wears really bright prints and colors. She can get away with it thanks to her petite body.

Shaun's head popped up behind his wife. "Mind if I join you ladies tonight?" he asked.

"Hi, Shaun," I said. "You can come, but you have to comb your hair first." His red hair was sticking out in every direction.

Shaun patted his head noncommittally. "But it's the same hairstyle your boyfriend has."

"Maxwell's hair is a little more," I paused, searching for the right word, "organized. He has a hairstyle. You have bedhead."

Shaun shrugged. "I had a little nap when I got home from work. The couch was calling to me. It's a haunted house, anyway, not a fashion house."

"Okay, but you're sitting in the back seat!" I smiled as Shaun complied, but as soon as we were all in my car, the topic quickly turned to the case at hand.

"The haunted house is off Waters Avenue, down on the Southside," Daisy instructed. "It's housed in an old warehouse from the mid-1900s, so goodness only knows who's haunting the place."

I screwed up my face in disgust. "Probably rats."

"Rats aren't known to caress women," Shaun said.

"I'd take a ghost over a rat any day."

"Me, too," added Daisy. "But still, I don't think I want to get felt up by something I can't see."

"How bad has the activity gotten?" I asked.

"I'm guessing pretty bad. When I talked to Matt last night, he seemed pretty concerned and wanted us to come out as quickly as possible."

"If their place is haunted, it could be good publicity for them," I mused.

"What are you suggesting?" I could see Shaun's thoughtful frown in my rearview mirror.

"Nothing. Just that we have to be really careful if we take on this case. These people are really good at making a place seem haunted, and I've heard of other tourist attractions that have faked hauntings just to get some good press out of it."

"And if our name is attached to an investigation, and word gets out that it was all fake to begin with, it would reflect badly on The Seekers," Daisy concluded.

We always try to maintain skepticism when we go on a paranormal investigation, but we agreed that we would have to be extra cautious at the haunted house. We didn't want to get duped by professional haunters.

It was almost dark when we pulled up in front of the old warehouse, but there were still a few people busy at work on the exterior, putting a fresh coat of paint on the sign that read, "Holy Terrors Haunted House."

As we walked toward the entrance, a young woman with bright blue hair spotted us. She climbed down the ladder she'd been using to reach the sign, threw her paint-brush on a drop cloth, and hurried over to us.

"Oh, thank goodness!" she said, extending her hand to Shaun. "We're so glad you're here. Azrael told us you'd be coming out tonight, and we are so anxious to know what's going on. Come on, I'll take you inside."

The woman kept up a constant stream of chatter as she led us through the main entrance. She introduced herself as Robyn and quickly launched into her own story.

"It's just weird, you know?" she told us as she skirted a row of cash registers and led us through a door painted to look like it was made of rotting wood. "I've worked this house for the past four years, and nothing has ever happened before. I mean, once in a while I get the creeps, but it's only natural when you're hanging out in the dark and all of your co-workers are in masks. Plus there are some really creepy people paying to come through here, and they're scarier than any of the staffers. So then this year, we come here to this new location, and suddenly it's not fun being back in the tunnels by yourself."

"Tunnels?" Daisy broke in.

"Well, not the underground kind. It's what we call the backstage passages in between all the scenes. It's how we get around this place without being seen. Anyway, there I am standing inside the tunnel that leads out into the cemetery scene, waiting for a cue to practice jumping out, and suddenly there's this hand grabbing my, um, well, my chest, and squeezing. It hurt. I thought another staffer was just playing a joke or something, but when I looked around I was alone. I've been pretty freaked out ever since. I mean, it wasn't even a romantic squeeze. It was hard. Oh, here we are."

We had been walking down a short hallway, and Robyn stopped before a door that was just plain black. We were in the backstage area that guests would never see, so there was no need for illusion. Robyn knocked sharply, then called out, "Az? They're here!"

The door opened wide almost immediately, and the man who referred to himself as Azrael loomed before us. He was easily six-foot four, and although he wasn't fat, he was far from small. He had long black hair that was curlier than Daisy's, and tiny wire-rim glasses perched on his hooked nose. His clothes were, I noted with no surprise, all black, right down to his studded boots.

"Welcome!" His voice matched his body, booming large and loud through the hallway. "I'm Matt. Come in, come in." As we filed in, Matt shook each of our hands in greeting. He might look intimidating, but he was all politeness with us.

Matt settled heavily into an old leather chair behind a cluttered desk. There were only two chairs for visitors, so Daisy and I sat while Shaun stood between us.

"Thank you very much for coming tonight," Matt began. "I can't tell you how much it means to me and my staff that you could come so quickly."

"If women are being harassed, then we want to help resolve this as soon as we can," Daisy said. "Why don't you tell us, in detail, what's been going on?"

"There's not much to tell. A lot of the staff members—especially the cast, who are often alone in the tunnels—started to feel weird being here. A few said they felt like they were being watched, and others said they felt like someone was there even if they were alone. I brushed it off as vivid imaginations at first.

"Two weeks ago, we started doing dry runs. That's when we set up where cast members will come out to meet their audience, how they'll make their entrance, how to time it, that sort of thing. On the second day, the girl who plays the possessed doll came to me, saying someone had put his hand up her skirt. Except when she looked, there was no one there. After that, other women on staff started to report similar things."

"Like me!" a voice piped up behind us. I turned to see that Robyn was still with us, standing in the doorway.

Matt nodded. "One girl quit already, and two more are threatening to. I can't lose staff, not this close to opening night."

"Matt, what do you know about the building itself?" I asked.

Matt spread his hands. "Not much. It was built in the mid-1900s and was once a factory of some sort. All I know is that we got a killer deal on the rent, and we needed more space so we could expand. This place fit the bill."

I nodded. "I'll look into it. Maybe someone died here at one time, and he's still hanging around."

Shaun suddenly turned to Robyn. "Did it feel like a male hand?"

Robyn thought for a moment before answering. Finally, she nodded. "Yes. It was a big hand, and strong. Why?"

"Betty just said 'he,' but for all we know it could be a female spirit."

"Whatever it is, I need it out of here, and fast." Matt was looking at us hopefully. "How soon can you come and do your investigation?"

Daisy had already pulled her calendar out of her purse while we'd been talking, but she was frowning. "We can't this weekend. We've got another investigation on Friday." She glanced at me and Shaun, adding, "That antique shop on Victory," before returning her attention to Matt. "And Saturday we won't have enough team members available."

I looked at Daisy questioningly. She mouthed, "Anniversary," and my eyes widened. "Already?" I asked. It was hard to believe that she and Shaun were already coming up on their first wedding anniversary. They had gotten married soon after we graduated college, but they'd been together for a couple of years while we were still in school. I couldn't picture either one with anyone else.

Now Matt was frowning, too. "We open next weekend. I'd sure appreciate it if you could come in before that. It's bad enough to have my staff members scared, but if something happens to a guest, it could mean a lawsuit."

"A sexual harassment lawsuit against a ghost?" I asked. I wanted to laugh but managed to keep a straight face.

Matt obviously saw no humor in it. "All it takes is for a guest to say she was harassed in my place of business. It doesn't matter by whom. Or what."

And however much the haunted house might want publicity, they certainly wouldn't want it at the expense of exorbitant legal fees. I mentally checked "looking for press" off my list of possible reasons for Matt's claims.

Still, I wasn't entirely convinced, and I turned to Robyn. "Did the first girl who was touched tell everyone else about it?" I asked.

"Yeah, everyone knew by the next day."

"Robyn, I don't mean to offend, but do you think hearing her story could have, like Matt said, caused some overactive imaginations?"

Robyn was shaking her head, and her lips were pressed into a thin line. "No way. No. It happened."

"I'm sorry. I had to ask. We have to consider normal explanations before pursuing paranormal possibilities."

"I understand. I know how it works with this stuff." Robyn's expression didn't soften. "But I can sense things. A spirit was there with me."

"You're a psychic medium?" Daisy asked.

"I wouldn't go that far. But I've always had that sixth sense. I get feelings when I walk into places. Sometimes empty houses feel crowded, or I'll start crying for no reason and then find out something really bad happened where I'm standing."

"You're sensitive." Daisy was nodding her head.

"I guess."

"Well, we still need to pick a date," Shaun interjected.

We finally agreed to come back the following Wednesday. I hated to book an investigation on a weeknight: it would mean a long, long day at work on Thursday. However, Matt said we could start early so we wouldn't have to be there too awfully late. He was happy we'd get in there before they opened up for the Halloween season.

Shaun wouldn't be able to attend because he had to get up too early the next morning. He worked for his dad's construction company, and they were doing a project out on Tybee Island. But as long as three of the four Seekers were available, we were willing to investigate. This time, that meant Daisy, Lou, and me.

Matt agreed to remain with us for the course of the investigation. He would act as a guide to navigate the backstage tunnels. I wasn't surprised when Robyn piped up with, "Can I come, too? Please?"

Daisy and I glanced at each other. You never knew how someone new to investigating would react, so it was a crap-shoot. If she really was sensitive, she could be a big help to us. On the other hand, she could be a liability and a distraction. Finally, I decided to defer to Matt. It was his haunted house, after all. "I'm okay with it, if Matt is comfortable with the idea."

Matt gave his consent before rising from his chair to end the meeting. He walked us all the way outside, where he shook all our hands again and thanked us at least three times.

"You'll be in good hands with these girls," Shaun promised.

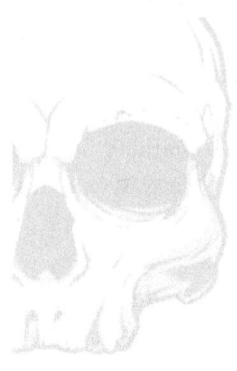

THREE

I got home from work on Friday, changed clothes (thank goodness I'd gotten two Seekers tees for myself, since I was wearing them so often), put fresh batteries in my camera and my tape recorder, and had everything in my "paranormal pack" by 5:30.

Too bad the investigation didn't start until eight. Other than Tuesday night's meeting at the haunted house, it had been a miserably boring week. Someone accidentally set off the fire alarm at work on Thursday, and that was as much excitement as I'd seen. I missed Maxwell, even though we talked on the phone at least once a day.

Even the number of calls and e-mails for The Seekers had tapered off after Monday's startling influx. I guess Maxwell had been right about interest slowing down as our investigation at the Everett-Tattnall House became old news. After two very quiet evenings, I was ready to check out the claims that we'd gotten from the owner of Low Country Antiques. The owner, an elderly yet energetic woman named Mrs. Strunk, had been hearing children's laughter throughout her shop. The occurrences, she said, began when she got a late-1800s steamer trunk that went up for sale in the front window. She wasn't bothered by the idea of having phantom children in her shop; she just hoped to find out who they were and why they were there.

Finally, at 7:30, I couldn't wait any longer. I got my case off my dining room table, gave my cat a pat on the head, and made the short drive to Low Country Antiques. It was in a strip shopping center about ten minutes from my apartment, and even though I was early, Daisy and Shaun had beat me there.

I walked inside the shop, which was small but far more organized than any other antique store I'd seen, and found Daisy politely admiring a collection of silverware that Mrs. Strunk was showing off. Shaun caught my eye and made a face. Antique stores were definitely not his thing.

I greeted Mrs. Strunk, whom I'd met during an earlier meeting with Daisy. She spoke about the ghosts in her store as if they were her own grandchildren. "The dears were quite rambunctious today, I'm afraid," she said. "Usually I only hear them when I'm alone, but they quite startled a young couple who were interested in the Chippendale wardrobe. Thankfully my customers weren't too frightened to spend their money!"

"Well, we'll get our infrared video cameras placed and get started, if you're ready," a voice spoke up behind me. I turned to see Lou Miles, who had crept in without any of us realizing it. He had to lean down to shake Mrs. Strunk's hand when he introduced himself. He was tall but, unlike Matt, he was so thin he looked almost gaunt. He had long, straggly hair, and was, quite honestly, the embodiment of an awkward tech genius.

"Hey, Lou," I said. I was trying to sound casual and hoped my nervousness didn't show. Lou and I weren't on the best of terms at the moment. He had serious concerns about me dating Maxwell. I really couldn't fault him for that since his reasoning was sound: Maxwell was a demon, and demons cause trouble. I knew that Lou had only expressed his displeasure since he's my friend, but unfortunately, the fact that I was still with Maxwell wasn't helping the growing tension between us. We'd only seen each other a few times since Lou had voiced his concerns, and the warmth and ease we'd once had was definitely strained.

"It's good to see you, Boo," Lou answered, looking at me with narrow eyes as if he were searching for signs of demonic influence. Well, at least he was calling me by my nickname. That was a good sign.

"I took a walk last night to get some exercise," I told him, "and I stopped in at the cathedral."

In answer, Lou reached out and squeezed my shoulder. "Good," was all he said. Lou was under the impression that demons couldn't enter churches or any kind of holy ground. He was also convinced that if Maxwell was using some kind of demonic persuasion on me, then I'd be adverse to religious sites, as well. To keep Lou happy (and to keep myself sane) I had promised to pop into the cathedral near my apartment on a regular basis, just to prove that I could.

Lou and Shaun set up one infrared camera so that it pointed toward the trunk, and they put a second camera at the back of the store so that it surveyed most of the showroom. Meanwhile, Daisy and I got our video monitor set up on top of the counter where the cash register sat. Mrs. Strunk pulled her chair out of her little office and made herself at home, perched so that she could see both the store and the monitor.

I volunteered to man the monitor with Lou. Since we were all in one room, there was no need to use our radios. In fact, since the only type of activity was aural, absolute silence was necessary. Daisy and Shaun settled onto the edge of the display area in the front window, next to the trunk. As soon as I flicked off the lights, we were all dead silent.

Things stayed that way for a good fifteen or twenty minutes. Finally, Shaun announced that he was going to try an EVP session. He brought out his tape recorder so he and Daisy could ask questions of the ghosts, pausing between each question to allow time for an answer.

Eventually, we fell into silence again. Mrs. Strunk, who had been quiet so far, spoke in a soft, maternal voice. "Children, it's okay to come out now. These friends just want to meet you."

Amazingly, as soon as she finished speaking, we all heard a quiet giggle. Lou and I turned to each other, and in the light filtering in through the front windows, I could see that his mouth was hanging open at least as much as mine.

A second, higher voice joined into the laughter. A boy and a girl, I thought, judging by the sounds.

"I brought something for you to play with," Daisy spoke to the unseen children. "I'm going to put this ball right here so you can roll it around."

Lou and I stared into the monitor so we could see the ball Daisy had placed next to the trunk. Absolutely nothing happened.

After another two hours, during which Lou and I sat by the trunk, then Daisy and I, then finally Daisy and Mrs. Strunk, all we had were those two quick bursts of laughter.

It was a pretty boring night, at least until we were packing up to head home. As I turned my tape recorder over to Lou so he could analyze the EVP session he and I had done, he casually asked, "So how are things with your boyfriend?"

"Really good."

"Demons are good at exploiting weaknesses. He might be treating you great right now, but he's studying you and looking for your vulnerable spots."

I sighed. "Thanks for the heads up, Lou." I couldn't help my sarcastic tone.

"It's true, and I'm only saying it because you're my friend." Lou thrust his hand toward me. "Here."

I opened my palm, and he dropped a silver necklace into it. "A St. Michael medallion? I'm not even Catholic."

"It doesn't matter. It's been blessed by a priest and will help keep evil spirits at bay. Please wear it. For me."

Lou looked so earnest that I couldn't help but agree. I fastened the chain around my neck and dropped the medallion inside my shirt. "Thank you, Lou."

"He won't like it." Lou sounded almost smug, like getting me to put the necklace on had been some small victory for him.

"I'd assume not." I paused, not sure what to say next. "I know you have my best interests in mind. Whether or not Maxwell likes it, this is a gift from a friend, and I'm going to wear it."

Lou smiled and abruptly changed the subject. "I'll call you once I've gone over all the recordings. Don't get your hopes up."

"I won't. Night, Lou."

I was thoughtful on the drive home. Lou frustrated me because he wouldn't avoid the subject of Maxwell's true nature. It was like he thought that if he warned me over and over again, I'd suddenly agree with him. I fingered the medallion idly as I fell asleep that night.

When I woke up in the morning, my hand was lying on top of the notebook that I keep in my paranormal pack. That's strange, I thought, I don't remember bringing it to bed with me.

I blinked a few times before I recalled that I hadn't even taken it out of my case after I got home. Yet there it was, lying open on my bed next to me.

And the writing on the page wasn't my own.

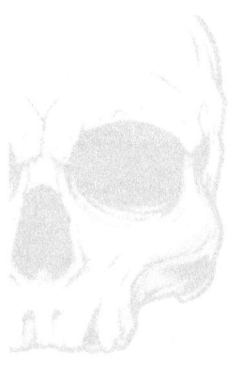

FOUR

The neat but close-set script looked very unlike my own scrawling handwriting, and no one had ever had access to that notebook.

I pulled the notebook toward me, propping myself up on my elbow to read it. "My dear Betty," it began,

"I was too anxious to see you to wait for my flight home today, so I thought I'd surprise you with a visit once you finished your investigation. I hope it went well and am looking forward to hearing all about it. I arrived here about four o'clock this morning with every intention of waking you in a most creative manner, but you were sleeping deeply and looked so peaceful that I didn't want to disturb you. I hope you don't mind that I curled up next to you and slept here for a few hours until it was time for me to be back in Washington. I'll see you tonight."

The letter was signed by Maxwell, and I had to shake my head at both his audacity and my bad luck in being such a sound sleeper. I was surprised that Lieutenant Griffin hadn't alerted me to Maxwell's appearance: seeing him materialize suddenly in my apartment must have been startling, even to a ghost. But, I conjectured, since Maxwell had given Lieutenant Griffin to me, my Spirit Sentry probably let Maxwell come and go as he pleased.

That thought was actually a little creepy. Was Maxwell

showing up in my apartment on other nights, while I unsuspectingly slept? Or was he popping in when I wasn't even home?

I had nothing to hide from him, so I decided that it really didn't matter. What did matter at the moment was getting some coffee into my system. I had a date with the Georgia Historical Society, and I needed to be completely awake.

I'd slept in, of course, since I hadn't gotten home until one in the morning the night before, and by the time I had two cups of coffee, showered, and got dressed, it was already eleven.

October had finally arrived, but the weather was still perfect for short sleeves, at least during the day. I took a sweater with me when I left for the Historical Society, though: that place was always ice cold.

I'd spent a lot of time in the Georgia Historical Society's building near Forsyth Park, and many of my Saturdays had been consumed by paging through dusty old records. I'm one of those weird people who actually enjoys researching properties that we investigate. Sure, it can be tedious, and it means a lot of solitude, but it's worth it for those blissful moments when some interesting tidbit of information pops up in an old newspaper or official document.

I walked to the Historical Society, and the woman sitting regally behind the desk in the historic records room greeted me warmly. "Back so soon?" she asked.

It was true; I had been there quite a bit lately. Even some of the cases that we ultimately had to turn down occasionally warranted a little research. Every time we told a prospective client that we wouldn't be able to handle their case—whether it was a time issue or the idea that their problems weren't of the paranormal persuasion—we referred them to one of several other ghost hunting teams in the area. I made a mental note to follow up with the other teams to see if they had gotten anywhere with some of the more intriguing cases.

My first order of business was to find out who had built the warehouse that Holy Terrors now called home, and when. I managed to find the building permit eventually: Morgan Manufacturing had built the place in 1947.

From there, it was time to search old newspapers for any news of accidents, deaths, or otherwise unusual activity happening at Morgan Manufacturing.

Finally, I found something on the front page of the December 12, 1959, edition of the Savannah Morning News. "Fire Kills 9 at Morgan Manufacturing," the headline screamed.

According to the article, an electrical fire had ignited a wooden bin that contained scrap metal. The flames went up the side of the bin and eventually reached the beams of the roof. Nine people were killed when the burning roof collapsed. The roof was rebuilt with sheet metal, and I guessed that it was the same one still in place now, though it had rusted over the years.

I made a list of all nine victims, then continued my search. When a newspaper from May of 1982 announced the company's bankruptcy and imminent closure, I gave up the search and glanced at the clock on the wall: five minutes until five. The Historical Society was about to close, so I rose and stretched. As I did, my stomach growled so loudly that even the woman working behind the desk looked around for the source of the noise. Embarrassed, I clamped a hand over my stomach before packing up my things. I had worked right through lunch, and I was starving.

Maxwell's plane was due in at seven, and we'd already made plans for a late dinner once he'd had a chance to go home and drop off his luggage. That gave me plenty of time to make a quick detour on the way home, swinging into a shop that has the best hummus and pita in the city. I took my food out to the nearest square and settled onto a bench. A pirate, a Confederate soldier, and a Victorian widow all passed me while I munched on my food. All, I assumed, were tour guides. Since it was a Saturday night and the busy fall tourist season, I knew the ghost tours would be out in full force. And if the people I saw weren't in costume for a tour, well, as long as no one tried to squeeze me into a corset, I wouldn't complain about anyone else's fashion choices.

I dropped the last few crumbs from my pita onto the ground for a pack of squirrels who had begun inching closer and closer to me with every bite I took. I had never thought that a squirrel could look murderous, but when they're used to being fed, they can be pretty aggressive. Better to share with them than face their wrath, I figured.

I took my time walking back to my apartment, enjoying the cooler air that the evening brought with it. The historic district really was crowded with visitors, and two people stopped to ask me for directions to different high-profile restaurants.

Maxwell called on his way home from the airport, promising to be by my side by 8:30. With time to kill, I called my mom, checked my e-mail, and paced back and forth between my living room and my dining room. Of course, with the tiny size of my carriage house apartment, I didn't have very far to pace.

By the time I heard Maxwell's knock on my front door (he usually arrives in a normal, human fashion), I had touched up my makeup, put on a slinky black dress, and pinned one side of my hair back with a little rhinestone barrette. I had also admired myself in the mirror for a few minutes.

I slipped into a pair of black heels and reminded

myself not to rush to the door. As much as I had missed Maxwell all week, I didn't want to seem too desperate. I took a deep breath and opened the door wide.

I found myself face to face with a bouquet of roses.

"Maxwell!" I squealed. "You're so sweet!"

The bouquet lowered, and Maxwell's face lit up in a brilliant smile. "I missed you."

"And I missed you. Welcome home." The words were barely out of my mouth before Maxwell had swept me up in an embrace, his arms nearly lifting me from the ground. His lips were every bit as eager as his arms, and he kissed me long and deep enough to make up for his absence.

Finally, Maxwell set me free and took a step back. "You look absolutely beautiful," he said.

"Thanks." I took the bouquet from his hand and motioned him inside. "And thank you again for these. They're gorgeous. Let me put them in water before we go out. So how was your trip?"

"Productive. I don't think I'll need to go back up there any time soon." Maxwell had a business dealing with importing and exporting. He continued to talk as he followed me into the kitchen, where I dug a vase out of a cabinet. "Something a little odd happened while I was up there."

"Oh?" I had started to fill the vase with water, but I shut off the faucet and faced Maxwell. Something about the tone of his voice put me on alert.

"Last night I took a couple of associates out to dinner. We were finishing up when I happened to look over at a table near us. There was a man sitting there alone. I think he was watching me. It's been a long time since I've felt that kind of a stare."

"Was he spying on you or something?"

"I think he was a hunter."

I sucked in my breath. Maxwell had told me there were

demon hunters out there, men who considered themselves on a holy mission to banish demons back to hell. "What happened? Did you say anything to him?"

"No. I took about five trains and one cab to get back to the hotel, but I can't be sure he didn't follow me." Maxwell paused, his expression thoughtful. "Hunters don't just show up. He knew what I am, and he had followed me there. I've dealt with enough hunters to know that much."

"How did he know you were going to be at that restaurant?"

"He may have followed me in, or somebody could have given him a nudge in the right direction."

Suddenly the note I'd gotten this morning made a lot more sense. "You came here in case he found your hotel room."

Maxwell nodded. "Partly. I also came because I missed you and was feeling a little mischievous."

I knew the serious part of the discussion was over by Maxwell's lighter tone, but I was still worried. "Maybe you need to take Lieutenant Griffin to your house for a while."

"No, he's better off here. Keeping you safe is important."

"And I'm sure he'll enjoy these while we're out." I arranged the roses in the vase and set it on my dining room table. I leaned over and breathed in their scent. "Perfect."

Dinner was perfect, as well. Maxwell took me to a Moroccan restaurant called Casbah. It was lavishly decorated, and we sat on low cushions to eat and watch as belly dancers shimmied their way around the room. The only downside to the entire experience was that I looked at everyone around us with suspicion. If a demon hunter had found Maxwell at a restaurant in Washington, was it possible he would trace Maxwell back here?

I soon realized that everyone seemed to be on a date, as it was all couples seated near us. I figured that demon hunters aren't the dating type and tried to push my fears out of my head. In fact, the only people staring at Maxwell were women, and I was becoming used to that. Whether it was his looks or some sort of demonic charm, he turned heads with ease.

When we got back to my apartment, Maxwell took me by the hand and led me into the bedroom. He kissed and nipped at my ear while one hand gripped the back of my neck. His other hand slid down to the hem of my dress. Maxwell usually moves gracefully, but this time he yanked urgently on the hem, pulling it up over my hips. He pulled my panties down with the same force, and I could hear his breathing become a soft moan in my ear. I shivered at the sensation, which only spurred Maxwell further.

Before I could react, he lowered me down onto my bed. I had the fleeting thought that I was still wearing my heels before Maxwell began kissing his way down my body. He kissed the insides of my thighs delicately, making me gasp in anticipation. Soon, his lips found the right spot between my legs, and his tongue darted out in a teasing little lick.

"Maxwell." It sounded like a plea.

I could feel Maxwell's lips turn up in a smile as they continued to press against my flesh, and when he began to lick again, he didn't stop. His tongue probed deeper as my moans of pleasure increased, and I began to rock my hips, pressing myself against him.

I was nearing my climax when the window blinds in my living room started to clatter as if someone were banging them against the window. Lieutenant Griffin was trying to warn us.

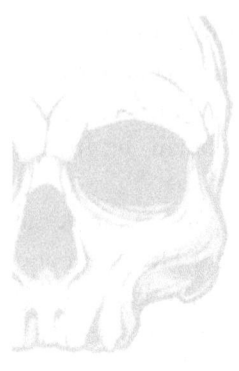

FIVE

Maxwell was instantly alert. He went to the doorway between my bedroom and the living room and stood with his shoulders hunched forward, like he might spring at any moment. I tugged my dress back into place as I came up behind him, peeking over his shoulder for any sign of danger.

"Lieutenant Griffin, is it someone outside?" Maxwell asked.

The blinds banged once in affirmation.

"Outside the front door?"

There was no response.

"The living room window?"

One bang.

"I'll be right back," Maxwell whispered to me. With a little "pop," he disappeared. I stayed right where I was, too afraid to approach the window. I listened closely, but the apartment was silent. No one was trying to force their way in, that was for sure.

In a moment, Maxwell materialized right where he had been standing when he left. "Where did you go?" I asked. My hands instinctively caught hold of his shirt.

"Outside to get a peek at our visitor. No one was there. He probably heard the Lieutenant's alarm and got scared off." Maxwell looked out at the empty living room. "Good

30

work, Lieutenant Griffin. You've done your job well tonight." When Maxwell turned back to me, his face was clearly worried.

"There was a pickup truck pulling away when I went out. I should have followed."

I frowned. "A truck? Was it a beat-up old green truck?"

"How did you know?"

I let out my breath in a huff, torn between relief and anger. "Lou drives a truck like that."

Now it was Maxwell's turn to frown. "Why would he be creeping around outside your window?"

I motioned Maxwell to the couch. I hadn't told him anything about Lou's concerns, but it was time to come clean. While I told him all the details, Maxwell absently rubbed his forefinger and thumb together, creating little sparks as he did so. It was a nervous habit of his that still made me a little wary.

My narrative ended when I touched the necklace Lou had given me. "He gave me this last night and begged me to wear it. Lou said it would protect me from evil spirits, but it obviously doesn't affect you."

Maxwell reached out and touched a finger to the medallion. "It doesn't affect me because you don't want it to. I expect it could protect you if you really needed it to, if you believed in its power strongly enough."

"Really? I always thought that power in objects like this was just superstition."

"The power is all here," Maxwell said, moving his hand to my temple. "You can focus that power and energy into an object. If that little charm has been blessed by a priest, as I suspect it has, then his power and energy have been focused on it, as well. You adding your own just compounds its potential.

"Right now," Maxwell continued, "I'd like to focus my energy on you. Whether that was your friend Lou or some hunter coming to visit, I'm not going to let anyone stop me from finishing what I started."

Maxwell had me in the bedroom again in a flash, but this time he slid his own clothes off and lay down on the bed. He pulled me up on top of him and I felt the now-familiar warmth that always spread through my body when he entered me. I moved my hips slowly at first, enjoying the slow pulsing of that warmth. The sensation grew hotter as I continued my motions, and I bit my lip to keep from crying out. It was pleasurable, but on the edge of becoming painful.

Maxwell grasped my hips and began to guide me in faster movements. The heat suddenly flared, and I threw my head back, a red haze tingeing my vision. At the same time, I felt my body swell to its climax in time with Maxwell.

The sensations coursing through me were all that I knew for a few moments, but soon I became aware that I was gripping Maxwell's arms tightly. I relaxed and leaned forward to rest against his chest. The heat had diminished into a soft, enveloping warmth.

Maxwell wrapped his arms around me and rubbed my back softly. Once I felt like my heartbeat had slowed to its normal pace, I rolled off him and snuggled into the crook of his arm.

I tilted my chin up so I could kiss Maxwell. "Good night," I mumbled, drowsiness setting in.

"Sweet dreams, Betty."

The next morning, I didn't let Maxwell leave until he promised to be extra cautious. I was convinced that Lou was the one Lieutenant Griffin had spotted the night before, but I didn't want to be caught off-guard in case I was wrong.

Once Maxwell left for his townhouse in the Victorian district of Savannah, I showered and slipped into a sundress. It was a little late in the season for it, but I was going dress shopping in preparation for the formal Halloween party at Fort Pulaski, and I wanted to wear something that would be easy to get on and off in a dressing room.

I picked Daisy up on the way to the mall, knowing I would need a second opinion. I hadn't worn anything approaching formal since my senior prom, and I doubted very much that big taffeta ruffles were in fashion anymore. Actually, I doubted they had ever been fashionable in the first place. Being a jeans and tee-shirt type, I didn't really know what I was doing when it came to dressing fancy.

I gave Daisy a hug and a peck on the cheek when she met me at the door of her house. "Congratulations on putting up with Shaun for a whole year!"

Daisy smiled widely. "I've been putting up with him for a lot longer than that!"

"You know what I mean."

"I know. One year of marriage down! We had the best dinner last night. We went to that place out on Tybee that Maxwell recommended."

"He'll be happy to know you liked it." I leaned over Daisy and shouted into the house. "Happy anniversary, Shaun!"

A quiet grumble was the only response I got. At my questioning look, Daisy laughed. "Somebody drank too much wine last night. Shaun's been on the couch since he woke up, and he'll still be there when we get back. Speaking of which, where do you want to go?"

"We'll look at some of the department stores at

Oglethorpe Mall, I guess. I don't have the money for something from one of those fancy little boutiques."

"No ruffles," Daisy instructed. I nodded grimly in agreement.

We were sitting at a traffic light when Daisy gave me a sidelong glance. "So, Lou called me this morning."

Uh-oh. "And?"

"He said that he won't be able to make it to the investigation at the haunted house. I'd called him about it last week, right after our meeting with Matt, and he'd said it was no problem. He wouldn't even give me a reason for not going."

"Daze, I think Lou is letting my relationship with Maxwell get to him."

Daisy's mouth opened in a wide "O" of surprise. "Do you mean Lou's in love with you, and he's jealous about Maxwell?"

I would have rolled my eyes at Daisy if I hadn't been busy trying to change lanes. "No, he's upset that I'm dating a demon, remember? But I think he's taking his displeasure to new heights." I briefly explained my security alert from the evening before, ending with Maxwell's description of the truck.

"That's too bad. I'm sorry he's so upset about it, though I can understand his worry. We all worry about you, Boo."

"I know. Considering someone tried to kill me in the past month and I'm dating a creature from hell, I can use a few worried friends. But spying on me is going a little too far."

"Are you going to confront him about it?"

I started to answer in the affirmative but shook my head. "Probably not. I don't think it will help anything. The only way to make Lou happy is to break up with Maxwell, which I don't plan to do anytime soon."

We drove in silence for a few moments until a thought struck me. "Damn it, now we're down to just the two of us for the Holy Terrors investigation! We need at least three of us to do a proper job."

"We'll figure something out," Daisy assured me. "It's not for another few days, so don't panic just yet."

I managed not to panic about the upcoming investigation, but looking at row after row of formal dresses in three different department stores had me nearly hyperventilating. At least two-thirds of the dresses were way too gaudy for me. Of the rest, most were far too revealing. I was all about looking sexy, but I didn't want to look like I charged an hourly rate.

Daisy and I were walking to the fourth, and last, department store at the mall when she stopped short. "Well, hey there," she suddenly said in a bright voice. I followed her line of sight to the entrance of the preppiest, most expensive men's store at the mall.

"Oh, no," I groaned under my breath when I saw who was coming out of the store. Daisy reprimanded me with a quick elbow jab to my ribs. I couldn't understand why, when she didn't like Carter Lansford any more than I did.

Carter stopped, quickly replacing his expression of surprise with a little smile. "Daisy, Betty, how nice to see both of you." Carter's soft Southern drawl would have been pleasant if it came from anyone else. But with his smile, his perfectly styled blonde hair, and his obviously expensive outfit, everything about Carter made me think of a politician out meeting his constituents. He oozed charm and charisma, but there was something slimy under that façade.

"We haven't seen you since that last press conference!" Daisy said. I was used to her greeting her friends enthusiastically, but Daisy's warmth toward Carter seemed a little over the top, even for her.

"East Coast Paranormal has been busier than ever," Carter answered smoothly. "It seems like every building in Savannah is haunted, and every owner wants us to come investigate. Besides," Carter looked directly at Daisy, "someone from your group very recently pushed me down a flight of stairs."

Daisy had the decency to look a little ashamed, but she still couldn't keep a straight face when she answered, "Are you still telling people it was a whole flight? Goodness, Carter, it was three, four stairs, max."

"So you admit you pushed me? The last time we talked about it, you claimed you lost your step and fell into me."

I'd heard this argument before, at Maxwell's house. I knew our conversation would go nowhere if they continued the subject.

"We've been busy, too," I finally spoke up. "I can't believe how many potential clients have been calling us."

Carter turned to me, and his anger at Daisy turned into sarcasm. "She finally speaks. I thought you were just ignoring me."

"You're impossible to ignore."

"Thanks, Boo."

"Have you had any good cases, Carter?" Daisy's voice was back to its ultra-perky pitch.

"Oh, yeah. We went all the way to Macon last weekend. It was a long way to go, but a team there needed extra help with a poltergeist. We made it into their local newspaper."

I was about to make a retort when Daisy said, "That's great! Do you have anything coming up soon?"

"Friday and Saturday nights of next weekend are booked. I've already got one case scheduled for the first weekend of November: the family wants to go on their annual vacation first."

"How very considerate of you," I mumbled, but

Daisy's voice overruled mine.

"You could investigate on weeknights," she suggested.

"That's next to impossible. Between my team members' jobs and the schedules of the clients, weekends are about all that works. You should know that."

"Well," Daisy reasoned, "maybe you could work on a case that doesn't involve your other team members."

Oh, no. I suddenly realized where Daisy's line of conversation was going. I couldn't just cut her off, but my brain was screaming, "No, no, no!" at her as loudly as it could. I hoped she'd suddenly develop mind-reading skills.

"What are you suggesting?" Carter asked.

"We're investigating Holy Terrors Haunted House this week, on Wednesday. We could use some extra help, and we'd love it if you'd come along."

Please have something else scheduled, I thought. Please!

"It sounds interesting," Carter said. "What's going on there?"

Daisy gave him the details while I stood mute. She even told him about Lou's sudden cancellation, leaving us without the necessary third investigator. We did need someone else to help us, and at least we'd worked with Carter before. He was arrogant, but I knew he wouldn't do anything too stupid during an investigation. Maybe working with him was a better alternative than bringing in another local investigator that we didn't even know.

I can't believe I'm talking myself into this, I thought.

Carter mulled over the question for a moment, then turned to me. "What do you think, Betty? Are you ready to team up again?"

I shrugged. "We do need the extra body," I conceded. "And since this entity seems to target women, it will be nice to have an investigator who's not at risk of being touched."

"In that case, I'd be happy to help you, just as long as I

get to team up with Betty." Carter's tone was triumphant. Daisy and I had just admitted that The Seekers needed help, and we (well, Daisy) had gone to Carter to get it. It actually made my stomach hurt a little bit.

I rolled my eyes. "Fine, Carter. But you should know that Holy Terrors doesn't want any press on this, so no press conferences."

"But it's such great publicity for them!"

"Not when women are being touched inappropriately."

Carter waved his hand casually, as if that were no concern. "Whatever. Maybe we can get some publicity afterwards, when we've gotten rid of the ghost."

One of the great things about Daisy is that she knows me really well. And at that moment, she knew I was about to blow up. She took me by the arm and steered me away, calling over her shoulder, "Great, we'll see you at Holy Terrors at six o'clock on Wednesday. Bye, Carter!"

When we were out of earshot, I turned to Daisy. "Why Carter?"

"We've done two investigations with him, and he was fine. Well, his investigating skills are fine. He's still a jerk. We needed someone, we know Carter, and I can't believe we just ran into him by coincidence." Daisy nodded her head. "We were meant to team up with him."

"Oh, no, don't you go implying that our fate is tied with Carter's! Yes, I'll agree with you that, jerkiness aside, Carter is the right choice to help us, but I'm still going to complain about it."

"I'm going to kill him with kindness," Daisy said. "Pushing him down those stairs was really satisfying, but I don't want to actually hurt him. I'm going to use a psychological attack: I'm going to be super sweet to Carter until he begs me to stop."

I laughed. "I almost—almost, but not quite—feel sorry for Carter."

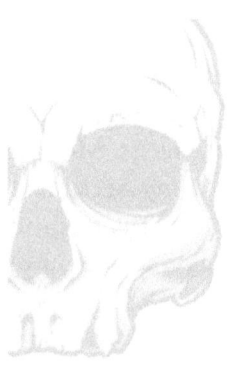

SIX

There were only two things that could make me feel better about teaming up with Carter again: finding the right dress for the party at Ft. Pulaski and a giant chocolate chip cookie from the mall's food court.

Luckily, I got both.

After our encounter with Carter, we went to the fourth department store at the mall, and I found the perfect dress after only ten minutes of searching through the racks. It was my size, it was slinky but not slutty, and it was on sale. Apparently it had been part of the spring line of dresses, and its spaghetti straps might be a little chilly out at the fort. But, I told myself, I could just cuddle up with Maxwell to stay warm.

Daisy paid for both of our cookies, since it was her fault I needed the comfort food in the first place.

I was feeling pretty good on our drive home: an investigation coming up in three days, a gorgeous new dress for a date with Maxwell, my best friend by my side, and a cookie in my tummy.

And then Lou called.

It wasn't so much that he called, but that he called Daisy and not me. Usually, Lou calls everyone after he's gone over all of our photos, video, and tape recordings from an investigation. Daisy never mentioned that she was in the car with me during her brief conversation with Lou, so I kept waiting for my phone to ring after she hung up. It never did, and I realized that Lou was distancing himself from me even further. My hand strayed to the St. Michael medallion that I was still wearing around my neck. Lou cared enough to give me the necklace, but not enough to make a simple call about evidence. That didn't quite make sense.

As it turned out, Lou didn't have much to report anyway. The two giggles we'd heard during the investigation were captured on Daisy's tape recorder, but otherwise there was nothing. Oh, well. At least Mrs. Strunk would be happy to know we'd captured the laughter of "her" children. I promised to go to the store with Daisy after work on Tuesday so we could give Mrs. Strunk a copy of the recording.

Daisy invited me to have a late lunch at her house. Afterward, I drove home to take care of a long to-do list that I'd been neglecting all weekend, starting with my overflowing laundry basket.

—————⚬⚬⚬—————

Monday promised to be a lot more fun than Sunday evening because Maxwell had offered to cook dinner at his place. I changed into jeans and a shockingly purple knit top (Daisy would have been proud) and arrived at Maxwell's around seven-thirty.

It felt weird to walk up the front steps of Maxwell's townhouse because I did it so rarely. Usually, I ended up at his house when he was driving, and we'd go in the back door after he parked in the old carriage house.

Maxwell's street was like something out of a period novel. It had cobblestone streets, huge oak trees dripping Spanish moss down onto the cracked sidewalks, and a deceptive quiet that belied the city all around us. Each of the wooden Victorian townhouses on Maxwell's block had been immaculately restored. His home was painted a deep burgundy and had three stories, though the ground floor was really just an aboveground basement.

I walked up the wide staircase that curved up to Maxwell's front door and rang the bell, feeling like a seriously underdressed Southern belle. Maxwell opened the door in a flash, as always: I've never gotten him to admit that he materializes to the door, but I have my suspicions.

I noted with some surprise that Maxwell was in jeans, too, which was rare. He ordinarily was dressed in a business suit or, at the very least, tailored slacks and a dress shirt. I wondered vaguely if he went to the grocery store dressed like that. Did he put on a three-piece suit to run out and buy toilet paper?

At any rate, Maxwell still looked handsome, and I felt a familiar warmth spread through me when he pulled me across the threshold and gave me a lingering kiss.

Maxwell led me down the long hallway and into the kitchen at the back of the house. We never ate in the formal dining room, and I'd only ever stepped foot in it once, just to take a look around. Instead, a small table in a nook of the kitchen served as our dining area. Maxwell pulled out a chair for me, and within short order I had a glass of wine in front of me.

"How was your day?" Maxwell asked. He was stirring a pot of something that steamed away on the stovetop.

"Busy, but good. My boss was really pleased with some text I wrote for the hospital's new website. I think he's coming around."

"That's good. I guess he never asks you about your investigations."

"No, he and I have silently agreed to have a 'don't ask, don't tell' policy. I just hope he doesn't find out about our investigation on Wednesday night. I'm sure he'd have a lot to say about me losing sleep on a weeknight."

Maxwell turned from the stove to face me. "Well, if he asks why you're tired on Thursday, just tell him that you were helping a friend who's dealing with sexual harassment issues at work."

"That's not a lie, exactly," I agreed.

"That's not a lie at all. You'd be amazed at how often I've been accused of lying, when in fact I've only been rephrasing the truth."

Part of me was tempted to ask for specific examples, but I knew better. That would only open the door to stories of Maxwell's demonic past, and I was perfectly happy not thinking about those things. "So what are we having for dinner?" I asked instead.

"Wiener schnitzel and spaetzle."

"German food? How did you learn to cook that?"

"I lived in Germany just before I came to Savannah, when it was still called the German Confederation. That would have been, oh, almost two hundred years ago. I developed a taste for their food, so when kitchens became more modern, I learned how to cook German recipes."

"Oh," was my only response. Maxwell had been living in human form on Earth for hundreds of years, but it was still weird to hear him talk about it so casually. He claimed that he couldn't remember what year he'd begun his human existence, but he had lived through the Dark Ages and then the Renaissance.

"What did you do before more modern kitchens came about?" I wondered.

Maxwell smirked. "I had someone do all the cooking for me. It made sense to keep help then, when just doing the laundry could take up a whole day. Now, though, I'm much happier on my own."

We kept up our casual chatter until it was time to dive

into the food. It was, of course, fantastic. After all, Maxwell had been perfecting his cooking for longer than I'd been alive. I would be a very plump ghost hunter if he fed me every night.

Dinner was winding down, and my wine glass was nearly empty, when Maxwell said, "I need to program a number into your phone. An emergency contact, if you will." He said it lightly, but I could see the seriousness in his eyes.

"An emergency contact for what?"

"You know, in case anything happens to me. Even if I'm out of the picture, it could still be dangerous for you if any hunters know about us. They could target you."

The thought made my arms break out in goose bumps. "Why? I thought they only banished demons?"

Maxwell spread his hands out in front of him. "The demon hunter network isn't all that great. One time, in England, three hunters all showed up to banish me on the same day. They started arguing about who should actually get to do the honors—the reward was high—and I was able to slip away while they fought.

"With that kind of disorganization, you can understand that if anything does happen to me, you need a way of getting word out that I'm gone, so you won't be harassed. You need to be safe."

"What am I supposed to do, send a notice to Demon Hunter's Monthly?" My joke was tinged with fear.

"Actually, you're not far off the mark." Maxwell got up and took my cell phone off the kitchen counter, where I'd laid it next to my purse. "I'm putting a phone number in here for Father Stockton. One call to him, and he'll get the word out."

"A priest? That seems like an odd emergency contact for you."

Maxwell punched the numbers into my phone while he

spoke. "Oh, he doesn't like me. The biggest price on my head right now comes from him. He has the ear of the hunters, though, and can ensure your safety."

I rubbed my hand across my forehead, willing it to unknot from worried concentration. "Okay." I stood and cleared the table, and after I rinsed the dishes, I turned to Maxwell. "I hope I never have to call him."

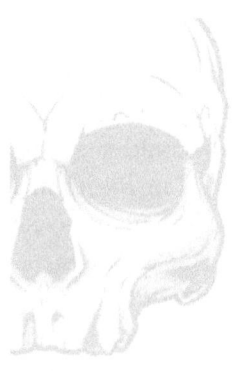

SEVEN

Carter Lansford looked very out of place. Wednesday night's investigation at Holy Terrors Haunted House had arrived, and once again we were all piled into Matt's office. Carter was perched on the arm of the chair I occupied, and his attention was torn between the hulking, black-clad form of Matt and Robyn's blue hair.

I found it vastly entertaining.

"Have you had any more incidents since we met?" Daisy was asking.

Matt nodded grimly and laced his hands in a tight knot on the desk. "Two. One was on Saturday afternoon. One of my staffers was putting some paint detail on a wall when she was grabbed. She was so startled that she fell off the ladder she was standing on and sprained her ankle. The other attack happened yesterday. It was the second time for that girl, and she quit on the spot. This is bad. We have to get rid of whatever this is."

"Of course," Daisy and I agreed in unison.

I filled the others in on what I'd learned at the Georgia Historical Society and suggested that whoever was harassing the women might be one of the nine victims of the fire. "I have a list of names, and we can address all of them during some EVP sessions," I explained.

There were only five of us, and without Lou there to

handle the tech side of things, it would take extra time to set up. We put a small folding table in the lobby of the haunted house (well, the entrance was decorated like the lobby of an old hotel, anyway), where we could keep the lights on. One infrared camera was placed in the tunnel separating the cemetery scene from the dungeon scene since Robyn and one other girl had met the ghost there. The second camera went in a scene decorated to look like a mental hospital. As far as I could figure from the article about the fire, it was where the roof had collapsed. It was possible that any lingering spirit would stick close to the site of his death.

Matt volunteered to man the monitor in the lobby. He wasn't afraid of being "attacked," as he kept calling it, since he was male. He was also used to working late in his office, so he wasn't at all creeped out by the scene around him: cobwebs, dead plants, portraits of exceptionally unhappy people, and even a suit of armor that, when activated, shook like it was possessed. Carter had unplugged the suit of armor five minutes after we started setting up. He claimed he didn't want the noise of it to distract Matt from his video monitoring, but I suspected that Carter was a little spooked.

With Matt settled behind the table, that left four of us. Carter had already claimed me as his investigating partner, and there was nothing to do but suck it up. Robyn went with Daisy, who was carefully explaining the rules The Seekers had for investigating.

Daisy and Robyn would check out the mental hospital first, leaving the tunnel to Carter and me. We were on the bare concrete floor of the warehouse, and the plywood walls were painted black. No frills backstage, I thought. I did a radio check when we got there and then called for lights out.

It was pitch black. There were no windows in the

tunnel to let in outside light, and it was absolutely, completely dark. I instinctively moved closer to Carter, just enough that my arm barely brushed his. I couldn't see him, but at least I could feel him sitting on the floor next to me. I'm not normally afraid of the dark, but this complete loss of vision made me jumpy.

"I think you should conduct the EVP session," Carter said. "Since you're a girl, the ghost might react better to your voice."

I fished my tape recorder out of my pocket and turned it on, using my memory of the buttons to find the right one. The little red light that came on shone like an evil eye out of the darkness.

"Hello," I began, "my name is Betty, and this is Carter. Is there anyone here with us? We're not here to harm you; we just want to speak with you."

I asked a series of questions, pausing between each. Finally, I said, "Carter, I'm going to turn on my flashlight. Watch your eyes."

I kept my hand over the flashlight's beam until our eyes adjusted to it. When I felt like I could use it without squinting, I opened my notebook to the list of fire victims. I began to address each person, one at a time.

"John Ayers, are you here with us? If you're John, can you give us a sign? Charles Cutter, are you here? Knock on the wall if you are."

I went through the whole list. Not only did nothing happen, but I didn't even feel like anything was going to happen. Usually, when there's paranormal activity, I can almost sense it: it's like the air is charged with electricity, and the tingling puts me on high alert. Right now, all I felt was mildly hungry since I hadn't eaten dinner.

Carter was apparently bored, too. He kept shifting, and finally he stood up to stretch.

"Well, we're off to an exciting start," he drawled.

No sooner were the words out of his mouth than we heard a short, high-pitched scream that echoed through the tunnel. I jumped to my feet as I brought the radio up. "Daisy?"

There was a pause that seemed to stretch for minutes until a shaky voice crackled out of the radio. "We're okay. Something touched both Robyn and me at the same time. Um, I think we need a break."

"Okay, let's meet in the lobby."

By the time everyone had regrouped, Daisy's initial shock was settling into determined anger. "That bastard grabbed my ass!" Her usually smiling face was flushed.

"What happened?" Carter asked.

"Well, Robyn and I were both feeling kind of strange," Daisy said. I remembered that Robyn claimed to be able to sense things, and I already knew that Daisy possessed some kind of heightened intuition. "And then I got that feeling I get, you know, right here." She was pointing at the nape of her neck. "Then, wham, all of a sudden there's a hand grabbing my backside."

"I felt it, too," Robyn chimed in. She seemed more spooked than angry.

"I haven't seen anything from the camera feed," Matt said.

"Let's all go back to that area," I suggested. "I want to see if anything will happen while we have a man with us. Or something resembling a man, at least."

Carter pursed his lips. "Gee, thanks."

I was about to make another snarky comment, but I stopped myself. Carter had, so far, been unusually nice to me. His arrogance often prompted him to belittle my ghost hunting techniques and, once in a while, he would make snide remarks about my personal life. Treatment like that made it really easy for me to be mean to Carter. But, since he had been fairly tolerable so far, I realized I ought to keep things nice between us.

"Sorry," I said flatly. "Old habit."

Soon the four of us were seated on the floor in a rough circle, surrounded by dummies in straitjackets, barred cells, and a hospital bed with wrist and ankle restraints. "That's where an actor will lay down. People think she's one of the dummies until they're right next to her, then she'll pop up and start screaming," Robyn said. "Like I screamed before. Sorry about that."

"It's okay," Daisy said, and I could tell by her tone that she had already said it to Robyn numerous times. "You have to work here every day, so of course you're a little more on edge."

"Let's get started." I radioed Matt, who flicked off the bright overhead lights so that we were once again in darkness. After sitting for a few moments in silence, something dim appeared on the far side of the room.

"What's that green light?" I said quietly. I pointed at it, though no one could see the gesture.

"Oh, that's glow-in-the-dark tape," Robin said. "It lines the exit routes in case of a power outage. I think it's a requirement or something."

Of course it was. "Right." Well, didn't I feel silly.

"Good one, Betty. You spied the paranormal tape."

"Shut up, Carter. You want me to bring up the dog?" Carter had mistaken a dog for a ghost at the Everett-Tattnall House. If he was going to break our little truce, then I'd happily fight back.

Carter flicked my ear, and I swatted my hand in his direction. "Quit it!" I swear, he and I are like a couple of twelve-year-olds the way we fight sometimes.

"Quit what?" Carter asked just as another flick landed on my earlobe.

"Stop touching my ear! How can you even see it in the dark?"

"Betty, um, I'm not touching you. I've got my camera in one hand and my tape recorder in the other."

"Then…oh. Take my picture, right now."

Carter did as told, counting to three first so I would know when to shut my eyes against the flash. He took a second one right after that for good measure. "Funny that something is just touching your ear, when all the other women are getting more personal treatment," he commented. "I guess the ghost doesn't find you as attractive."

"Well, I'm sitting, and my arms are crossed over my chest. That rules out the really offensive spots." The hair on my right arm was raised, and I felt something like friction against my skin. It was the same feeling I got if I was in a crowd and had to stand really close to a stranger. "Whatever is here, he's definitely invading my personal space."

"Can you come over here?" Daisy asked, her voice coming from my left. "I have my hand out, see? You can come and hold hands with me, and you can talk into my tape recorder."

The strange feeling against my right side instantly dissipated. "It's coming your way, Daze," I warned.

"It's okay," she continued. "I'm not mad at you for grabbing me the way you did before. Not anymore, at least."

After a few moments, Daisy giggled nervously. "It feels like someone is brushing their fingers against my palm. It kind of tickles."

I suddenly shivered and glanced around, even though I couldn't see anything. Carter must have had the same sensation because he said, "The temperature is dropping." I saw the soft glow from his digital temperature gauge illuminate his face. "It was seventy-four degrees when we came in here. It is now sixty-two."

There it is, I thought. That tense feeling in the air that indicates something paranormal is going to happen. It was like anticipation made palpable.

"I don't like this." The voice was Robyn's, but it was barely above a whisper.

"Hold my hand, honey," Daisy said, her tone calm and matronly. "Betty, why don't you try your list?"

I pulled out my flashlight and notebook. "John Ayers, are you here with us?" I began again. "If it's you, please squeeze my friend's hand again."

Nothing.

"Charles Cutter, are you here? Please make a noise or touch one of us."

Again, nothing.

"Martin Dyer, if you're here, please make yourself known."

This time, something happened.

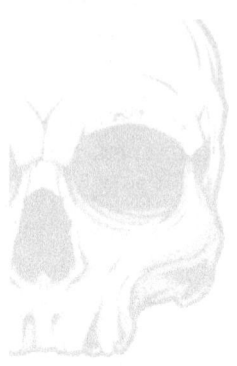

EIGHT

Robyn gave a long scream, so loud that I dropped my notebook and clamped one hand over my ear.

"No way!" she shouted. "This is insane! I am not going to sit here and go through this again. I'm out of here."

"Daisy, go with her," I instructed, passing my flashlight to her. "Carter and I will wrap up."

Robyn was already on her feet and hurrying toward the nearest tunnel when Daisy called after her. "I'm coming, too. You're not supposed to be alone, remember?"

A string of expletives came out of Robyn's mouth, but she slowed down to allow Daisy to catch up. We could hear her shouting all the way down the tunnel, not at Daisy, but about the ghost. "Unbelievable! Why would I keep working in a place like this? Who does that to a girl? This is completely ridiculous."

Finally, Robyn's voice faded away. Shortly after, Daisy's voice came over the radio. "We made it back to the lobby. Matt and I will do what we can to calm her down."

"Thanks, Daze. And Carter and I will do what we can to get this spirit out of here."

That was the only cue Carter needed. "Martin Dyer," he spoke loudly, like a commander addressing his troops, "you are dead. You died in this warehouse in a fire, and your spirit is all that is left. Are you aware that you are dead? If your answer is yes, squeeze Betty's hand."

"Gee, thanks," I mumbled, but I extended my hand anyway.

"It's okay," I added, addressing the ghost. "If you know you are dead, squeeze my hand."

There was no response, and when I told Carter, he continued. "Martin, you and eight other workers were killed when the roof collapsed in this spot during a fire. You are the only one left, and it's time for you to move on. Do you understand me?"

The air around my hand became ice cold. "That's a yes."

"You have nothing to be afraid of. Better things await you than staying in this dark warehouse until the end of time. You should see a light and hear the voices of friends and family calling to you. Do you see it?"

I felt a feathery touch on my palm.

"They love you, and they will help you. Go to them."

I felt one last touch on my hand, softer than before, and I realized the rest of me felt warm. "Carter, what's the temperature in here now?"

There was a pause, then, "It's back up to seventy-four."

That tense, anticipatory feeling was gone, too. "I think our work here is done," I said hesitantly.

"Yeah."

Carter and I rose, and I called Matt on the radio to have the overhead lights turned back on. I scooped up Daisy's tape recorder, which she'd left recording when she had gone after Robyn. When we re-emerged in the lobby, Daisy appraised us with a stern face. "You two look whipped."

"I am pretty exhausted. And it's not even eleven o'clock yet!"

Carter was smiling, but he looked tired, too. "I think

that ghost was pulling all the energy he could, and we were unwitting donors. On the upside, I think he's gone."

"Really?" Robyn was sitting against the wall, and Daisy's arm was tight around her shoulders. Robyn's heavy black eyeliner was smeared from crying, but she looked much calmer.

Carter and I explained what had happened after she and Daisy left, and I tried to describe the lighter feeling I got after Carter had spoken to the spirit of Martin Dyer. Robyn was nodding her head in understanding. "I have a question, though. Why was he always grabbing at the girls here?"

I looked at Carter, and we both shrugged. "He could have just been a pervert," Carter said.

"Or maybe he was frustrated that no one could see or hear him, and he was lashing out in any way he knew how," I added before turning my attention to Matt. "The only real way to know if we've been successful is to see what happens over the next few days."

"We have rehearsals tomorrow. The night before we open is when friends and family can get in for free to be our test audience. I'll tell the staff to be alert but not to worry. Thank you."

"Don't thank us yet," I warned. "We'll call and follow up with you after tomorrow's rehearsals."

I was pretty thoughtful while we packed up our equipment. Robyn refused to leave the lobby, but Matt happily assisted us. Carter rolled up one extension cord before giving up and checking e-mail on his phone. I was tempted to reprimand him but checked myself. First, he wasn't part of The Seekers, and he was doing us a favor by standing in for Lou that night. Second, he had been impressive in the way he spoke to Martin's ghost.

I had never expected to be impressed by anything Carter did, other than his skill at promoting himself and the way his blonde hair always looked so perfect, no matter what was going on. But the way he'd spoken to Martin with such a perfect blend of authority and kindness had surprised me. Not only that, but it had apparently worked. He had made Martin understand he was dead and had gotten him to cross over with almost zero effort. At least we hoped that was the case.

There was one more surprise waiting for me, though. We all walked out together, and Matt locked the doors of the warehouse behind us. He thanked us profusely before walking Robyn to her car. When it was just the three of us, Daisy stood on her toes and wrapped her arms around Carter's neck. I didn't know who was more shocked: Carter or me. He stood stiffly for a moment, then awkwardly wrapped his arms around Daisy's waist. I stifled a laugh when I saw the bemused expression on his face.

When she finally pulled away from him, Daisy was smiling sincerely. "Great work tonight, Carter. Thank you for helping us."

"Uh, you're welcome." Carter looked slightly defensive, as if Daisy's thanks might be followed by an insult or even a shove to his chest.

Daisy hugged me next, promising to call the next evening. She was clearly anxious to get home, probably since she hadn't seen Shaun all day due to their overlapping schedules.

That left just Carter and me, and I decided to take the plunge and broach the subject that had been occupying my thoughts. "Carter, I have a question," I began.

"I don't know why she hugged me, either."

"No, not about Daisy. About what you said to Martin's

ghost tonight. How do you know that his spirit will be better off by crossing over?"

Carter was quiet as he considered his answer. "Well, spirit communication has affirmed that they see a white light and hear the voices of people they knew and loved. Martin affirmed it tonight. That, in itself, seems to indicate a better existence than being stuck in this world. Psychic mediums say the spirits they talk to are happier in that plane, that their fear and sadness are gone."

"But what if they can only talk to the people who go on to that particular plane? What if there are other planes that aren't so bright and welcoming, where communication with the spirits is cut off?"

"I guess it's possible, but evidence doesn't seem to support it."

"And what if Martin was a bad man? He was going around harassing the women here, so who knows what he did in life. What if he isn't heading for a better place?"

"You're talking about hell," Carter said. "You should ask your boyfriend." Carter knew that Maxwell was a demon, but he was all too aware of Maxwell's destructive power to ever voice distaste for our relationship.

"We try to avoid those kinds of topics. But he did once describe hell to me." Showed me was more like it, complete with the smell of sulfur and the sensation of being burned alive. I suppressed a shudder at the memory. "It was awful."

Carter's voice was quiet when he spoke again. "What am I supposed to do? Tell a spirit like Martin that eventually he'll be judged, and he might wind up in hell? Nobody would ever cross over."

"And if they did, they might change their mind and do everything in their power to claw their way back to this life. I wouldn't blame them."

"If we're all waiting to face our judgment someday,

wouldn't you rather wait with those who have died before instead of haunting an old, dingy warehouse?" The usual arrogance was gone from Carter's face, and he looked at me earnestly. He actually cares about these ghosts, I realized. Ghost hunting isn't just a way for him to be in the spotlight.

"I would. It's nice to think there's somewhere safe and carefree waiting for us. All right, let's get out of here. Thanks for helping us, Carter."

"You're welcome. And Betty, keep faith that our spirits go on to something better after this world. How could you ever live if you believed someone you loved was in hell?"

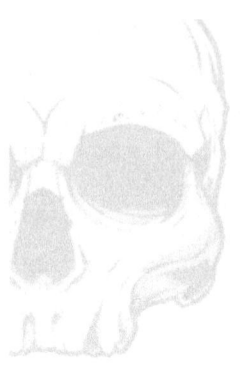

NINE

I was downright perky at work on Thursday morning. Between starting our investigation at Holy Terrors early and our quick results, I had gotten home and in bed before midnight, so I wasn't tired like I had anticipated. Our apparent success had also put me in a good mood.

Often, people who ask us to come investigate don't want to get rid of any spirits; they just want confirmation that the haunting is legitimate and not all in their heads. The typical manifestations—footsteps, knocking, the occasional object moved from its spot—aren't threatening, and families learn to live with their spectral houseguest quite happily. It's rare that someone is so scared, or the ghost so offensive, that we're asked to help it cross over. I knew Carter had dealt with more cases like that since violent ghosts usually resulted in better stories. He already had one book out and was probably collecting material for another.

I didn't even complain when I had to spend an hour standing at the copy machine after lunch, making copies of a presentation one of our doctors was giving at a medical conference. Normally, I'll stop off at our receptionist's desk on the way to the copy room to vent a little. I hate making copies.

Instead, I just leaned over her desk as I passed by, teasing her with a whispered, "Hey, Jeanie, I've got a hot date on Saturday!" Our receptionist is the queen of office gossip, and she loves hearing about my dates with Maxwell.

Thinking about Maxwell reminded me that I needed to straighten up my apartment before he came over that night. We tended to get together every couple of days, which was perfect. As much as I adored him, I wasn't ready to spend every waking moment with him. I still had time for my ghost hunting and for myself.

After work, I got my sweeping and organizing done quickly, and I was ready to go when Maxwell knocked on my door at seven. We walked a few blocks to a nearby café and sat at one of the tables on the sidewalk. Maxwell looked otherworldly, the way the candle on the table threw shadows under his cheekbones. I reached out and caressed his cheek, and Maxwell turned his face to kiss my fingers softly.

"Sometimes I just can't believe you're real," I said.

"I'll be happy to prove that I am, if you're in doubt." Maxwell's tone was suggestive, and he caught my hand in his and held it tightly.

"You probably should, just in case. I'm just amazed at how lucky I am. And yes, I know how cliché that sounds, but I've got you, I had a great investigation last night, and I've got a party at Fort Pulaski to look forward to."

"How was your investigation? You were such a tease on the phone last night, telling me I had to wait until tonight to get the details."

I filled Maxwell in, and he was as surprised with Carter's finesse as I had been. "You mean he didn't even offer to give the ghost an autograph?" Maxwell asked.

"He did really well. It kills me to admit that."

"I can imagine."

"All I'm waiting on now is a call from Holy Terrors to tell us how their rehearsal goes tonight. I'm hoping it's nice and quiet, and that the guests are screaming instead of the employees."

By the time Matt called me, Maxwell and I had eaten, walked back to my apartment, and he was nibbling on my neck before saying good night. I was going to let the call go to voicemail, but Maxwell could see the anticipation in my eyes. He pulled back. "Answer it. Let's find out if Carter's a hero."

He was. Matt told me enthusiastically that there had been no problems whatsoever during the last-minute set dressing during the day or during the rehearsal that night. "And my girls are all so relieved," Matt finished.

"Have you told Carter?"

"I just got off the phone with him. He mentioned something about a press release, but I wasn't quite sure what he was talking about."

Of course Carter wanted to publicize his success. "Well," I began, but Matt cut me off.

"How about we discuss it tomorrow night? If you're all free, I'd love to have you come through the haunt as my guests. Bring a date, if you like."

I glanced at Maxwell. "I'd love to, Matt. Thanks. I'll see if I can talk my boyfriend into it."

"Be there at nine. Skip the line and ask for me at the cash register."

When I got off the phone, Maxwell instantly resumed his nibbling, moving his lips down to my collarbone. "Want to go to a haunted house tomorrow night? I promise to scream myself hoarse," I said.

Maxwell brought his face up so it was just inches from mine. "You're not afraid of me, but you get scared by people in masks?"

"Oh, no," I told him seriously. "It's the guys with the chainsaws that really freak me out."

When Matt had mentioned a line, I'd pictured a couple dozen haunt fans lined up outside of Holy Terrors. It was more like a couple hundred. Thankfully the parking lot outside the warehouse was ample, but we were parked about as far away as possible. I knew Holy Terrors was popular, but most places didn't get crowded until closer to Halloween. I figured that everyone must be anxious to get into the spirit this year.

Maxwell and I had driven to Shaun and Daisy's house so we could carpool with them. Both of the guys were looking forward to seeing the place since neither of them had visited before. Daisy regaled us with the story of her spectral harassment, as she was calling it. It hadn't been funny at the time, but her retelling had all of us laughing.

As Matt had instructed, we skirted the long line and went right inside the lobby. A skinny guy wearing a pair of little horns on his head stood behind the cash register. "You can't cut in line," he said in a bored voice.

"We're here to see Matt. He's expecting us," Daisy said, giving the guy her most charming smile.

"He's popular tonight," he said, pointing his thumb over his shoulder. "Go on."

We went into the hall, but we couldn't get into Matt's office because someone was taking up the entire doorway. He seemed to be coaxing someone, or something, inside the office. "Yes, that's it, just a little more casual. Perfect, perfect."

Undeterred, Daisy walked up to the man with a polite, "Excuse us, please." A heavyset man with a balding head and lime green polo shirt turned to Daisy. "Just one minute, ma'am. We're about done at this location."

That's when I noticed the man had a camera in his hands. I'd been so distracted by the color of his shirt—

which made him look like a giant frozen margarita—that I'd overlooked his camera.

"Carter!" I shouted. I didn't have to peek over the photographer's shoulder to know he was in there.

"Betty, perfect timing. Want to come get in the picture?" Carter's voice drifted from Matt's office.

"No."

After a few more shots, the photographer backed out of the doorway to let us in. Carter was dressed like he was attending a business dinner, right down to his shiny silver cufflinks. It wasn't exactly haunted house attire.

"Now, what's all this?" I asked offhandedly. I knew full well what it was. "I thought you had an investigation tonight, anyway."

"Cancelled. And I'm here since Matt agreed to let me alert the Savannah Morning News to their haunting. It will be great for the newspaper's Halloween-themed editorial." Carter looked extremely proud of himself.

So did Matt. He was clearly enjoying the attention, and I knew he'd be grateful for the publicity now that sexual harassment wasn't the scariest thing happening at Holy Terrors.

I sighed. If Matt was on Carter's side in this, then I couldn't argue. "We just finished the interview," Matt told us eagerly. "We're going to get a shot of me outside with that big gargoyle in the background. If you'll all excuse me a few moments, I'll be right back."

Matt hustled out, his large frame eclipsing the photographer's.

I instantly turned to Carter. "This was a Seekers investigation," I began, "so shouldn't we have had a say in whether or not we publicized the case?"

"You did have a say, and you said yes." Carter's voice was smooth.

"No one asked me about this," I sputtered. It wasn't

that I minded a little press—after all, it was good business for Matt—but at least it should have been run by The Seekers first.

"I gave the okay." The quiet confession came from Daisy, who was looking at her shoes. "Carter asked, and I said it was all right. It's the least we can do to thank him for helping us."

"Oh. Well, um, okay, then. Sorry if I got a little shouty there, Carter."

"Not at all." The only time Carter's voice lost its haughty edge was when he extended a hand to Maxwell. "Good to see you again."

Shaun diffused the tension between Carter and me when he tossed a CD onto Matt's desk. "There's an EVP on there that you will all enjoy hearing. I expect our friend from the newspaper will be impressed, too."

"Shaun got home from work yesterday and immediately started going through my EVP sessions," Daisy explained.

"Lou didn't want them?" I asked.

"I didn't want to bother him since he wasn't able to make it to the investigation." Daisy's tone was light, but her implication was clear: Lou didn't want to be involved. He was slowly pulling away from The Seekers and from me. Maxwell seemed to sense my disappointment, and he reached over to take my hand. I squeezed his fingers. I hated losing Lou like this, but I didn't want to lose Maxwell, either.

Matt and the photographer returned in short order. Matt settled back into his spot behind his desk, and the rest of us were squeezed uncomfortably opposite him. I was going to introduce Maxwell and Shaun, but Daisy was the first to speak. "We got an EVP!"

"A what?" The photographer looked mystified by Daisy's excitement, and she quickly explained how tape recorders sometimes catch phantom voices that we can't hear with our ears. Meanwhile, Matt put the CD in his computer and turned his speakers up all the way.

I jumped when Carter's voice boomed from the speakers. "You are the only one left, and it's time for you to move on. Do you understand me?"

The answer came quickly, but quietly. "Yes, yes, yes, yes." It sounded male.

"A ghost said that?" The photographer's eyes were wide.

Matt played it again. "That's so great! Did you get anything else?"

Shaun shook his head. "That's it. Still, considering this ghost seemed to communicate exclusively through touch, it's nice that we were able to capture his voice."

"Can I put this on our website?" Clearly, Matt had an eye for publicity like Carter.

"Of course," I said. "We just ask that you include a link to our website."

"Done! I'll do a whole page about the haunting and the investigation. We can put the EVP on there, and we'll put the logo for The Seekers up. This is great! Thank you!"

Matt rubbed his hands together eagerly, like a villain hatching a plot. His voice dropped, and he raised one eyebrow. "And now, it's time to spook my spook hunters! Are you ready for Holy Terrors?"

"That's my cue to leave." The photographer reached over Daisy to shake hands with Carter and Matt, then made a hasty exit. The rest of us eagerly filed out of the office. I'd much rather be screaming than crammed shoulder-to-shoulder with Carter.

Matt led us right to the wide archway that marked the beginning of Holy Terrors Haunted House. I heard a few people at the front of the line grumble a little when we cut in front of them, but Matt cleverly turned it into a chance to pitch his haunt. His voice took on a deep, ominous tone, and it carried well into the crowd of people. He had chosen to wear a black suit tonight, complete with tails, and a top hat was perched on top of his curly hair. When he spoke, he resembled the master of ceremonies from some evil carnival.

"Ladies and gentlemen, we beg your forgiveness! We enter Holy Terrors before you not for our own entertainment, but for your safety! These brave souls are ghost hunters. They faced peril when they came here two nights ago, encountering a most aggressive spirit. Have they banished him successfully? Or do we all go to our doom? If we do not re-emerge, then you will have your answer!"

A smattering of applause followed, but most people laughed, assuming, no doubt, that it was all part of the show. "You think I am in jest!" Matt continued. "This lady here," he gestured grandly at Daisy, "was grabbed fiercely by the spirit on her, well, there are younger guests here, so we can't tell you that!"

I didn't need to glance at Daisy to know that she was blushing bright red. Carter was smiling widely, while Shaun and Maxwell were both laughing heartily.

With that, we stepped through the archway of the haunted house with laughter. I love getting caught up in the fantasy of haunted houses, though, so I was the first person to shriek when a figure rushed at us out of the darkness.

As we moved through the house, I recognized Robyn when she popped out of a tunnel as we shuffled through the cemetery scene. She hung back and shadowed Shaun, following him quietly as we passed into the next scene. He was unaware that she was still behind him until he turned to speak to Daisy and was met instead with a shock of blue hair and a face painted to look like a rotting corpse. He gave a loud shout that made even Robyn giggle.

I was so absorbed in the gory, gloomy scenes around me that I didn't even notice Maxwell's discomfort until we were about halfway through. He was holding my hand, and I had a tight grip on him so we wouldn't get separated in the dark passages. When we came into a scene that was better lit, I finally relaxed my hand, only to realize that Maxwell's own grip had become possessive. I glanced at his face, and in the dimness he looked nervous, his eyes sweeping back and forth.

I halted. "What?" I asked quietly.

"I don't know. Just a weird feeling. There are a lot of places to hide here."

Suddenly the made-up zombies, vampires, and psychos didn't seem so amusing. I swiveled my head, expecting someone to loom up out of the darkness at any moment. "A hunter?" I whispered.

Maxwell gave me a long look before answering. "I'm probably just being paranoid. You'd think that after so long, I wouldn't let it get to me anymore."

There was a high scream behind us, and I jumped. It was just the next group of guests coming through. "Come on," Maxwell said. He pulled me behind him as we hurried to catch up to the others.

When we finally came up behind Shaun and Daisy in the mental hospital scene, I overheard Shaun ask, "Isn't this where the ghost grabbed you? Did it feel something like this?"

Daisy's loud shriek, followed by a quick smack to Shaun's arm, confirmed that he was, in fact, trying to recreate our investigation.

I was doing all right until the very end of Holy Terrors, when three men in hockey masks chased after us with chainsaws. I know they can't hurt us and that the chainsaws don't even have chains on them. Still, Maxwell learned to his great amusement that they really do freak me out.

We all thanked Matt for inviting us out, then decided to go get dessert and coffee at a diner nearby. Maxwell and I hadn't even eaten dinner yet, but everyone agreed that ice cream was the best thing for our throats after screaming our way through Holy Terrors. Even Carter came along at Daisy's urging, though he looked mildly offended at having to eat at a run-of-the-mill diner.

After we ate, Shaun drove us all back to his house, where Maxwell had left his car. When Maxwell and I were finally alone on the drive back to my apartment, I brought up his nervousness in Holy Terrors. "Do you get feelings like that often?" I asked.

"Don't worry about it, Betty," Maxwell said, putting his hand on my thigh. He squeezed gently and looked over at me seriously. "I think that encounter at the restaurant in D.C. spooked me more than it should have. Usually, a hunter will act quickly after tracking down a demon. Instead, there has been nothing. Maybe he was able to track me in D.C. but lost the trail when I came home. He doesn't know where I live."

I nodded and felt comforted. The more time that went by, the less Maxwell needed to worry.

Too bad Maxwell wasn't finished. His final word was ominous.

"Yet."

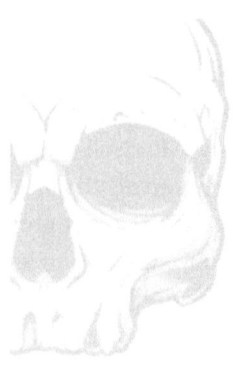

TEN

When I awoke on Saturday, I was determined to spend the entire day preparing for my date with Maxwell at Fort Pulaski. I'd never been to a formal party like this, but between it and Holy Terrors, it seemed like the perfect way to kick off the Halloween season. After all, Fort Pulaski was notoriously haunted by soldiers who had died there. If Maxwell had anything to do with it, we'd probably see a ghost or two before the evening was over. He seemed to have the ability to not only communicate with them, but to make them materialize on command.

After the prerequisite coffee, I pulled my new dress out of the closet and admired it for a while. It had been on sale but still wasn't cheap, and I was glad I already had high heels and jewelry to go with it. If I'd had to buy the whole outfit, I might have been eating ramen noodles for a couple of weeks to make up for the expense.

I was going to splurge on a little pampering, though. I put the dress back into the closet, opting for casual clothes. I slid into a pair of flip-flops to walk to the salon a block from my apartment. Daisy was meeting me there, and we were going to get manicures and pedicures.

Daisy didn't have a special occasion; she just liked to spoil herself. I tended to overlook a lot of things, like pretty fingernails, but Daisy considered them a must. She had always had a stronger girly streak than me.

We had fun gossiping with each other while we sat in the pedicure chairs. "I can't believe Carter went with us for dessert!" I said.

"I think I'm in danger of not hating him," Daisy replied glumly. "I've really got to stop being nice to him, because whenever I am, he goes and does something nice in return."

"What do you mean?"

"Well, I asked him to help us out at Holy Terrors, and even you have to admit he did a terrific job."

"And he and I got along better than usual that whole night."

"Yes. I still can't believe I hugged him. But anyway, I have to tell you what happened at the diner last night. Did you know he offered to put me in touch with his dad? Not only that, but when I woke up this morning, Carter had copied me on an e-mail to his dad, recommending me to him."

Daisy worked for a legal firm as an assistant. Like my job, it was entry-level since it was her first "real" job out of college. But Daisy was really organized, easy to get along with, and good at what she did. She also didn't much care for her employers, since they were, in her words, "damn ambulance-chasing blood-suckers."

I suspected Carter's father might be a bit of a blood-sucker himself if he was anything like his son, but he was a very well-respected lawyer in Savannah.

"Wow," was all I could muster.

"I know, right? Carter asked me last night what I did for a living. When I told him, he said his dad was looking for extra help and he'd recommend me if I was interested. Of course I said yes, but I didn't expect Carter to actually follow through."

"How did I miss all of this?"

"Carter was kind of quiet about it. I think he brought it up while you were defending the merits of *Grease 2* to Shaun."

"Can you blame me? It's a great movie. As for Carter, I'm glad he's helping you out. Just keep an eye on him. He's a slippery one, and if he can use his connections to give you a hook-up, he can probably use them to make your life miserable."

"That's my only concern." Looking at Daisy, though, she really didn't seem concerned whatsoever. Her eyes were closed, and the corners of her lips were turned up in a smile. She had the right idea. I put my own head back against the chair and enjoyed the feeling of the water swirling over my feet.

Daisy and I grabbed a light lunch after our time at the salon. I now had lovely burgundy nails all around and was feeling quite luxurious. Daisy had opted for a sedate, pale pink on her fingernails, but her toes sported a bright orange. She claimed it was a Halloween decoration.

When I got home, I showered and dried my hair. I wasn't quite sure how to make it look appropriately formal to match my dress. I could have pulled it up if it was long like it used to be, and I was still angry at the demon who had burned off my hair. It had taken a few weeks to get used to my new short style, but I finally agreed with everyone else that it was flattering on me.

I took a break from playing with hairstyles when I realized it was only mid-afternoon. While I had planned to spend all day getting ready, the truth was that I had lots of time on my hands.

I made up for it by settling onto my couch, my cat

Mina curled up by my side and *Casablanca* playing on the TV. I fell asleep long before the famous good-bye scene between Ingrid Bergman and Humphrey Bogart, and when I finally awoke, the clock read six.

I bolted upright. Six o'clock already! I'd gone from having too much time to barely enough. Maxwell was going to pick me up at seven, and he was always prompt.

My make-up was easy enough, but I was still at a loss as to what to do with my hair. Finally, I decided to stick with something simple. I used a curling iron to roll the edges under and pulled one side back with a black satin barrette.

After I dressed, I took a long look at myself in the mirror. My dress was a deep green velvet, and it hugged my curves right down to my ankles. Between the spaghetti straps and the long slit up the back, though, I was still showing some skin. Zipping myself up had been a bit of a challenge, but I'd managed it without too much awkwardness. My jewelry was simple: a gold and emerald ring I'd gotten from my grandmother, little gold teardrop earrings, and a matching necklace.

Maxwell knocked on my door at seven o'clock exactly. I slid into my strappy black heels and gave my hair one last fluff before I answered the door. Maxwell looked absolutely gorgeous. As if to punctuate his arrival, the sky lit up just as I opened the door. A rumble of thunder followed.

"You wore that suit the first time we met," I commented. Tonight, Maxwell had paired the three-piece pinstripe suit with a black dress shirt and a black tie. His face was even paler than usual against the black of his suit and his hair. "And you're still just as handsome."

"You," Maxwell said, leaning in to kiss me, "look stunning." He took my hands and held me at arm's length. "Very sexy. I just hope you don't wind up soaking wet."

"I didn't realize there was rain on the way." I could

deal with wet. Getting struck by lightning, however, would be a bad way to end a date.

"We'll take shelter in the officers' quarters if we must!"

There were a few more flashes of lightning during our drive to Fort Pulaski, but the storm was far off on the horizon. Maxwell drove his Audi R8 like he was in a race, keeping up light conversation with me the entire time. It wasn't until we parked and Maxwell opened the door for me that I doubted my choice of footwear. The gravel parking lot was an obstacle course for me in my heels. Then again, what else could I have worn with this dress?

I had never visited the old fort after dark. During the day, it looked gray and dreary, its stone walls looming up like a medieval castle. As we took the walkway that led to the entrance, the fort rose from the surrounding marsh in bright orange and green. Instead of feeling spooky, the colored spotlights gave Fort Pulaski a festive feel. I took a deep breath. The humidity was still there, but there was the distinct crisp feel of fall in the air. "It's Halloween season," I said quietly.

"Most people only celebrate the holiday on one day. I like your notion of celebrating for a whole month."

"Halloween is the season of fantasy. You can dress up in costume and become anyone or anything you like. It's the one time that you're allowed to believe in monsters, zombies, and vampires."

"And demons."

Other couples and groups of party-goers were walking near us, and I was relieved to see that my dress was right in line with what the other women were wearing. A woman ahead of us wore a pink spangled dress that reminded me of a princess costume. Instead of feeling underdressed compared to her, I just thanked my lucky stars that I didn't look like the disco version of cotton candy.

We crossed the bridge over the moat that surrounded

the fort and passed under the tall stone entrance. The brightly dressed, smiling woman who took our tickets as we passed stood out in stark contrast to the torch-lit passage under the fort's walls.

Inside Fort Pulaski, thousands of orange and white party lights crisscrossed the open parade ground. There was already a sizable crowd, and people were grouped around small portable tables. Big band music played over speakers.

Before I had time to take in any more of the scene, a waiter approached us with a silver tray. "Pimiento cheese balls?" he droned.

I happily took one off his hands and realized there were waiters roving everywhere. Maxwell clearly had the same thought as me: he moved in the direction of the waiter carrying a tray of wine glasses.

All of the rooms within the fort's thick walls were open, and we wandered through, sipping wine and looking at recreations of Civil War-era life at the fort. "No wonder Lieutenant Griffin was willing to relocate to my apartment," I commented. "That parade ground must have been brutal in the summer."

"I'd take the heat over the mosquitoes from the marsh any day."

I screwed up my face. "Yuck." A sudden thought struck me as we looked at a collection of rifles. "Maxwell, where were you during the Civil War?"

Maxwell gave a short, mirthless laugh. "That's a very long story. I promise to tell you when we have a lot of time on our hands."

A voice suddenly echoed through the fort, keeping me from asking any further questions. We followed the sound to the parade ground, where a man in a tuxedo was standing on a small stage, speaking into a microphone.

"They are here to help us kick off the Fort Pulaski

Halloween Ball in authentic style!" he was saying. The crowd began to applaud as five men dressed in Confederate uniforms came onto the stage. They marched over to a cannon, which I had assumed was just for show.

I could hear shouted commands as the re-enactors worked. With a distinct cry of "Fire!" the cannon boomed, and a puff of smoke billowed out of the end. There was no actual cannonball, but it was an impressive demonstration. The assembled partiers cheered, and Maxwell and I joined in.

The music started up again, and Maxwell and I walked through the crowd. I accommodated each waiter we encountered, so by the time we reached a buffet table, I was feeling full already.

Maxwell helped himself to the crab cakes and a hearty portion of shrimp and grits, then balanced a biscuit on top of it all. I decided I still had room for the offerings on the dessert table. We sat down at an empty table and ate leisurely, watching the people strolling past.

More than a few people stopped to greet Maxwell. Most were older men who walked up with wide smiles and hands extended. "Mr. Damon," said one, "it's been too long. You look so much like your daddy."

I gave Maxwell a sidelong glance at that comment. Since he'd been in Savannah off and on over the past two hundred years or so, it made sense that some people would figure he was the son of someone they'd known years before, someone who looked exactly the same as Maxwell. It was also odd to hear anyone use Maxwell's last name. He had introduced himself to me as simply Maxwell, using his demon status as a sort of title.

Maxwell was gracious to everyone who stopped to say hello, standing and shaking hands while flashing his most charming smile. It was clear that he was well respected by each person who stopped.

When there was a lull in the string of visitors, I leaned toward Maxwell and spoke in a low voice. "You're popular."

"My work as a demon is a lot easier to accomplish when everyone likes me," he answered. "Honestly, though, most of them I know through my business, and a few of them I genuinely like. Come on. Let's take a stroll."

I readily agreed, and we made our way up to the ramparts, where we could see the Savannah River shining beyond the walls of the fort. The storm was much closer now, and the wind blowing across the ramparts was damp and cool. I shivered.

Maxwell slid his coat off and draped it around my shoulders. It was warm from being against his body all night, and I pulled it close around me.

I stopped to take in the view, ignoring the lightning that I saw streaking across the sky. Maxwell observed me for a moment, then turned me toward him. He wrapped his arms around me.

"Having fun?" he asked.

"Yes. This is wonderful. Thank you for bringing me."

"You're welcome." Maxwell fell silent, but his blue eyes were intent as he gazed at me. When he spoke again, his voice was quiet but firm. "I love you, Betty."

In that moment, I felt like the entire world had stopped around us. I couldn't hear the music from the parade grounds or feel the wind of the approaching storm. Early in our relationship, Maxwell had hinted that he was falling in love with me, but he'd never spoken the words.

"I love you, too, Maxwell." I knew I sounded breathless.

Maxwell kissed me softly, then took my face in his hands. He looked at me searchingly again, but this time his lips were turned up in a content smile.

Eventually, Maxwell broke the silence. "Should we get out of here?"

I nodded reluctantly. It was better to leave now and beat the storm, I knew, but I hated to end such a perfectly romantic moment. Maxwell seemed reluctant, too, and he was slow to take my hand and turn toward the stairs.

Leaving was easier said than done. The parade ground stood between us and the fort's entrance, and at least half a dozen people stopped Maxwell to offer a greeting. "You know everyone!" I whispered to him after the Chief of Police had finished saying hello.

Maxwell waved it off with a casual, "It's Savannah."

The walkway outside the fort was empty, and we strolled slowly toward the parking lot. Maxwell was still holding my hand, and I leaned my head against his shoulder.

The wind calmed momentarily, and then I felt a sudden, sharp breeze across my face. Something dark shot past my line of vision at the same time I felt Maxwell's entire body tense. He released my hand and shoved me in the direction of the parking lot.

"Run, Betty!"

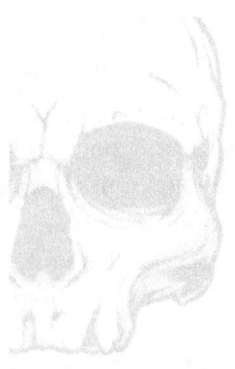

ELEVEN

I didn't know what was happening. I stumbled a few steps away before turning to look back. Maxwell was facing the edge of the marsh off to his right. There, fifty yards away, a man stepped out of the shadows. His broad frame was covered by a long coat, and he had a bow in one hand. His other hand reached over his head to pluck another arrow from his quiver.

A demon hunter.

He ran swiftly despite his size and began to close the gap between himself and Maxwell.

"No!" I shouted. I should have stayed quiet, but the sound escaped my lips before I could react.

The hunter's gaze flicked briefly from Maxwell to me.

"She's not the one you want," Maxwell's voice was loud, but I could hear the fear in it. "She's innocent."

Maxwell turned and ran across the grass toward the river. I knew he was trying to draw the hunter away from me. I also knew that I should run, just like he'd told me to.

Instead, I stood, too shocked to move, as the hunter sprinted after Maxwell.

Whether by chance or some demonic ability, Maxwell quickly outpaced the hunter. The hunter finally stopped running, but he didn't give up. He dropped to one knee and fitted his arrow to his bowstring.

I lunged forward, shouting incoherently and praying I could reach the hunter in time. But over the sound of my shouts and my feet scrunching through the grass, I heard a soft "thwap." The arrow rocketed out of the bow and sailed for Maxwell. I watched, horrified, as Maxwell's body crumpled, disappearing over a small rise in the ground.

I ran right past the hunter without stopping. I had no regard for him or for my safety. My thoughts were focused on nothing but Maxwell.

When I crested the rise, I saw Maxwell's clothes lying in a heap on the ground. The arrow had pierced his vest. Maxwell's body was gone.

I stopped running so quickly that I lost my balance. I fell to my knees next to Maxwell's suit. My boyfriend had been banished back to hell.

I screamed his name, even though I knew he had passed beyond hearing. I yanked the arrow out of his vest and threw it away from me, gasping as if it might harm me, too.

All sense of time left me as I began to sob.

I don't know how long I sat there, completely enveloped in my grief. Gradually I became aware that it was raining and that my hair was already soaked. I remembered the demon hunter, but when I looked up, he was gone. He must have left, satisfied with his success.

My first coherent thought was that I needed to call the police. My second thought was that it would be pointless to do so. What would I say to them? That my demon boyfriend had completely disappeared at the hands of a rogue archer?

I took a deep breath and was trying to form a plan when a faint buzzing noise began to emanate from the pile of clothes on the grass. Maxwell's phone was set to vibrate.

I pulled the phone out of his pants pocket and saw a

text message displayed on the screen: "Betty, call me right now." The message came from someone named Tage.

I did as the message instructed, and a deep, slightly accented voice answered my call. "What happened?"

"Um…" I hesitated. I didn't even know who this guy was, so I didn't know if my story would sound outrageous to him.

"I'm a friend of Maxwell's. A demon."

"It was a hunter." I swallowed to hold back more tears. "He came out of nowhere, and Maxwell's gone."

"What weapon did the hunter use?"

"An arrow."

"Dipped in holy water and blessed by a priest, no doubt. I'm sorry, Betty. Maxwell has mentioned you many times."

"How did you know something had happened?"

"I just knew." Tage stopped abruptly, and after a short pause he continued. "It's hard to explain. Betty, I need you to do something for me, okay?"

"Okay."

Tage instructed me to pick up anything of Maxwell's, as well as the arrow. Remove the evidence, I thought. "Are you okay to drive?" he asked. "You need to get out of there without anyone seeing you. Let everyone assume you and Maxwell left together already. Otherwise, there would be too many questions."

I agreed, but Tage had more instructions for me. "Drive to Maxwell's house, and leave his car there. I'll call a cab to meet you. You have a fireplace?"

"Yes."

"Take Maxwell's things and the arrow, and burn them. If anyone asks, you tell them that Maxwell drove you home, but you never heard from him after that. Let people think what they want. It's better for them to think Maxwell left town than to suspect anything supernatural was going on. Do you understand?"

"Yes." One-word answers seemed to be the most I could manage.

Tage asked for my phone number, then ended the call with a curt, "Good luck, Betty."

I gathered Maxwell's wet clothes and easily found his keys in a pocket. I knew I had thrown the arrow somewhere off to my right, down the slope that led to the fort's moat. I slipped off my heels and added them to the pile of Maxwell's clothes. It was still raining lightly, and I began to despair of ever finding the arrow in the dark grass when I stepped on something hard and slender. It was the shaft of the arrow.

With everything in hand, my next step was to get away before anyone could see me. No one was on the sidewalk, and I was thankful that the rain was keeping people inside the fort.

The parking lot was still full of cars. Someone was pulling out as I neared, but it was otherwise quiet. I slid into the driver's seat of Maxwell's car and put my bundle on the seat beside me. I started the car, cranked up the heat, and started to cry again.

Finally, I sat up straight and took a few deep breaths. I had to get this over with.

The drive back to Savannah took much longer than when Maxwell was behind the wheel. Eventually, though, I pulled into the alley behind his townhouse.

What was I supposed to do with the car keys? They wouldn't burn in a fire, and I hated to just leave them in the car. I decided to take them with me. I could figure out what to do with them later.

A taxi was just pulling up when I emerged from the garage, just as Tage had promised. I had put my shoes back on, but I had taken off Maxwell's jacket so I could wrap the arrow in it. The taxi driver stared as I slid into the back seat. I knew I presented a horrid sight: I was wet, my mascara was probably running, and I suspected that my eyes were red from crying.

Thankfully it was a short drive to my apartment, and I paid quickly so I could get away from the driver's scrutinizing gaze.

I had every intention of collapsing onto my couch to cry some more when I got inside my apartment. The small puddle I left on my floor while locking the front door behind me made me think twice. Besides, I had to carry out Tage's instructions. The sooner I got it over with, the better. At least that's what I told myself.

I changed out of my wet dress, exchanging it for a pair of sweatpants and a tee-shirt. I would deal with my hair and makeup later.

There were just a few pieces of firewood left over from last winter. My fireplace was tiny, but after some work I had a small blaze going. The heat felt good after the chill I'd gotten in the rain.

I threw the arrow on the fire first. I was anxious to be rid of it. Maxwell's clothes were much harder for me. His vest was on top of the pile, but I folded it neatly before tossing it into the fire. When I began to fold his shirt, I heard the ping of something small hitting the floor. A bullet.

But the hunter had used an arrow. Where had this come from? After a moment, I realized it was the bullet Maxwell had taken for me on our first real date. He'd saved my life that night, and although his wound had healed overnight, the bullet had remained inside his body. The memory brought a fresh wave of grief, and I hugged the shirt to me. I had a wild urge to dry it and keep it, but I knew I couldn't. It went on the fire, too.

I saved the bullet. I figured it wouldn't melt in the fire, anyway, and it was a reminder of Maxwell's affection.

When I was done burning his clothes, I was left with Maxwell's car keys, his wallet, and his phone. His wallet contained very little: his driver's license, business cards, two bankcards, and cash. Four hundred and twenty-three dollars, to be exact.

I threw the cash, bankcards, and business cards into the flames. I wasn't sure a leather wallet would burn, but I chucked it in, too. Maxwell's driver's license, on the other hand, I kept. I would hide it somewhere along with his car keys and phone. It was silly, I knew, but I couldn't bring myself to destroy something that had Maxwell's picture on it. And handsome demon that he was, he managed to look good even in his driver's license photo.

Now that my task was done, I allowed myself to sink onto the couch to cry some more.

When my tears finally dried, I didn't feel any better. In fact, I felt worse. My energy was gone, and I didn't even feel like sitting up. I was absolutely wretched.

I called Daisy. I hated to disturb her at such a late hour, but I knew she would understand. I'm not sure what I actually said to her on the phone, but I knew she understood two things: I was upset, and it had to do with Maxwell.

Daisy got to my apartment just as I finished hiding Maxwell's keys, license, and phone. I put the bullet inside my jewelry box, where I could see it every day.

I shuffled to the door and opened it to find a very anxious Daisy. Her eyes were already filled with tears even though she hadn't heard my story yet.

Daisy had me sitting on the couch with a hot cup of tea in my hands in no time. It felt good not to have to actually think for a few minutes. Once she was next to me, one arm over my shoulders, Daisy simply said, "Tell me."

I didn't leave out a single detail. Even in my grief, I was glad that Daisy knew about Maxwell's nature so that I didn't have to hide anything from her. She cried with me as I choked over my description of Maxwell's body disappearing.

When I was done, Daisy sighed. "I don't even know what to say. I'm so sorry."

I laid my head on her shoulder. "I'm just glad you're here."

We were quiet for a few moments before I spoke again. "He told me he loved me tonight."

"Of course he loved you. For a demon who was supposed to be creating chaos, he did an awful lot to make your life simpler. You know, like saving your life once or twice."

"And I loved him."

"I know, honey."

I yawned. "Daisy, I'm going to attempt going to bed. You should probably get home; it's late."

"Silly Boo, I'm staying with you tonight. But you're not allowed to go to bed until you've showered. Your cheeks have black stripes."

Daisy went so far as to turn on the shower for me. I stayed in there until the water started getting cold.

I was more tired than I had realized. After Daisy tucked me into bed and headed for her makeshift bed on the couch, I closed my eyes and didn't awake until daylight was streaming through my window.

My dreams had been filled with arrows and screaming, but at least I'd made it through the night.

Daisy stuck around for most of Sunday morning, but I was ready to be by myself for a while. She went home, promising to call that evening, and I promptly went back to bed. I wanted to be alone, but I didn't want to do anything productive. I deserved at least one day to grieve.

I skipped work on Monday, too. I had intended to go in, knowing that getting back to my normal routine would be good for me, but when I got up Monday morning, after another nightmare-filled sleep, I felt physically and mentally exhausted. I called in sick. It wasn't far from the truth.

It was bad enough that my boyfriend was gone, but having only Daisy and Shaun to mourn with me made it that much harder. Under normal circumstances, I knew I'd have a flood of people coming to offer condolences and casseroles. Instead, I was home alone, with no one calling to check up on me. Well, Daisy called three times, but otherwise I had no contact with the outside world on Monday.

Finally, I called my mom. I told her that Maxwell and I had had a great time at Fort Pulaski, but that I hadn't heard from him since. He wasn't answering his calls, I explained. I felt absolutely terrible about lying to her.

After that conversation ended, I felt doubly worse: now I was grieving, and I was a liar. I did the only thing I could think of that might make me feel better: I walked over to the cathedral on Abercorn Street. The usual tourists who visit the historic church were already gone for the day, and there were only a handful of parishioners scattered around. I sank into a pew and put my head down on my folded hands. I prayed for Maxwell.

I didn't even know what I was praying for, really. If he had been banished to hell, then what could be done about it? Still, I had to try. It was the only thing I could do.

When I had finished my silent prayer, I looked up and caught sight of a statue of Christ standing tall between two stained-glass windows. It was on the side of the church, in the shadows. My eyes followed the statue from its upraised hand down to its sandal-clad feet. A small altar filled with lit candles sat below, and someone was kneeling there, his head bent in prayer.

As I watched, the man stood up and turned to leave. I cried out when I saw his face and clamped a hand over my mouth.

It was the demon hunter who had killed Maxwell.

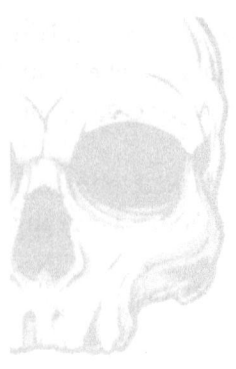

TWELVE

If I hadn't cried out, the hunter probably wouldn't have noticed me. Instead, his eyes went right to my face. I quickly looked straight ahead, anxious to avoid meeting his eyes. My hands were locked tightly together.

Maybe he wouldn't recognize me. I was still wearing the same sweats and tee I'd gone to bed in on Saturday night, though I'd at least had the decency to put on a bra before leaving the house. My hair was lank, and I wore no make-up. I doubted very much that I looked anything like I had at Fort Pulaski.

Please don't see me, I thought desperately.

I saw him out of the corner of my eye as he turned and began walking straight toward me. Was he going to kill me for associating with a demon? Not in a church, surely.

The hunter entered the pew directly ahead of me. He walked slowly until he was nearly in front of me. I bowed my head again, and now my prayer wasn't for Maxwell, but for myself.

The wooden pew in front of me squeaked as the hunter sat down, his broad back just a few inches from my head. He angled his body toward me and spoke in a whisper. "It had to be done. For the glory of God and the good of His world. He was a demon, Betty."

The demon hunter knew my name. How had he discerned that? I nodded curtly, too afraid to meet his gaze.

"I know you loved him, and I'm sorry you had to witness his banishing. Believe me when I say you are safer now. You won't understand that because you didn't understand him." The hunter's tone was actually sympathetic.

He thought I was unaware of Maxwell's true nature. It was, I decided, best to let him continue thinking that.

"It's good that you are here. Let your soul find comfort in the presence of God."

With that, the demon hunter stood and walked away. I remained where I was for a long time after that.

Running into the demon hunter had reminded me about Maxwell's warning that I could be a target, too. If that hunter had recognized me, then who else might?

As Maxwell had instructed, I called the number for Father Stockton that he had programmed into my phone.

The man who answered the phone sounded a hundred years old.

"Hello, is this Father Stockton?"

"Yes, yes, but speak up, please."

I raised my voice. "My name is Betty Boorman." I paused, not sure what to say after that. Introducing myself to a priest with "I used to date a demon" might not go over so well. Instead, I said, "I used to date someone named Maxwell. I believe you know of him."

"I do. That creature has been eluding me for fifty years."

"Not anymore. A hunter found him on Saturday."

I could hear the priest's grin over the phone. "Oh, he's been banished, has he? It's about time. The hunter must be working for some other priest. Otherwise, I would have been notified."

I bit my lip. The priest's obvious joy made my heart ache even more. "Could you please tell your hunters the news? I don't want to be in danger."

"Why, are you a demon, too?" Now the priest's voice was sharp.

"Certainly not."

"You just don't want to be used as leverage, especially against a demon who's already back in hell, where he belongs."

"Yes, exactly."

"Very well. I'll tell my network of hunters. And Miss Boorman?"

"Yes?"

"Try to be more particular about your boyfriends in the future."

I heard a click, and the conversation was over.

I crawled out of bed reluctantly on Tuesday morning. I had to go back into work. I knew I'd feel better if I was busy and if I wasn't in my tiny apartment, where everything made me think of Maxwell. The dining room table reminded me of the dinner I'd served him, the couch made me think of curling up with him to watch TV, and the bedroom, well, I was trying not to think about that, actually.

My throat was sore. It was ironic, since I'd called in sick on Monday, and now I really was feeling under the weather. I was sure it stemmed from sitting out in the rain on Saturday and the chill I'd gotten from my wet clothes.

I sipped hot tea while I worked and gave the same "I'm fine" answers to everyone's inquiries about my health. I was blessedly busy: the distraction was exactly what I needed to get my mind off Maxwell.

Going home meant diving back into all those memories of Maxwell. I hadn't had a lot of boyfriends, and I'd certainly never had one disappear like this, whether by death or banishment. I wondered how long it would take before I stopped feeling so miserable.

Daisy, at least, knew I'd be wanting some company. She had called earlier in the day to invite herself over. She promised to bring dinner and some cheer.

Daisy arrived with a container of homemade chicken soup, chicken fingers from The Burglar Bar, and a gallon of chocolate fudge swirl ice cream. "The soup is for your sore throat, the chicken fingers are your favorite thing on the menu at The Burglar Bar, and ice cream makes you feel better when you're suddenly single," Daisy explained. It was a bizarre mix, but I couldn't argue with her logic.

I told Daisy about the demon hunter and the priest in between bites of chicken fingers. She was indignant. "Who do these people think they are, anyway?" she asked.

"Holy men."

"Oh, right. I guess you were kind of sleeping with the enemy."

I snickered. Only Daisy could make a joke about my banished boyfriend and actually make me smile. I spontaneously reached across the table and took her hand. "Thank you, Daze. I guess, if there's any silver lining, it's that I don't have to worry about having a demon in my life. Lou really had me worrying about what kind of adverse effect it would have on me."

Daisy looked at me thoughtfully and gave my hand a squeeze. "Someday you'll find positive outcomes for all of this. Right now, there's nothing wrong with just being unhappy."

"I know. No matter how upset I am, though, I can still

recognize that life without a demon is going to be a whole lot easier and a whole lot less of a moral dilemma." Of course, knowing that didn't make me feel any better at the moment. I had once broken up with Maxwell because he was a demon—and because I'd learned some of the evil things he'd done in the past—and I'd felt awful then, too. It was too bad that logic and love didn't go together better.

I felt a little healthier at work on Wednesday, both physically and emotionally. I was still having nightmares about Maxwell's banishing, but focusing on getting back into my normal routine was keeping me from sinking too low.

I had no plans for Wednesday night. I considered driving down to the Southside to have dinner with my mom, but I didn't quite feel ready to face her. Lying to her on the phone was bad enough; doing it in person would be excruciating.

Instead, I grabbed a book and walked over the The Big Bean Theory, a nearby coffee shop. It got me out of the house, it was cheap, and I could lose myself in someone else's drama for a while (in this case, Miss Elizabeth Bennett's).

I dove right back into my own drama when I got home and found Lou sitting on my doorstep. When he saw me approaching, he stood and stepped back so I could unlock the door.

"Lou, I didn't know you were coming over! You should have called." It was odd to find him waiting for me, but it was good to see him, at least.

"I tried to call but it kept going to voicemail. I was a little worried." At my odd look, Lou shrugged. "Daisy told me what happened." Lou had a sympathetic look on his face, but I knew he was inwardly relieved.

"Oh. Sorry I missed your calls. I was at the coffee shop

and left my phone in my purse. I hadn't expected anyone to be calling me."

I unlocked the door and waved Lou inside. "You want anything?" I asked.

I was already pulling out a pitcher of sweet tea when Lou answered. However much our relationship had changed lately, I knew his preference for tea had not.

Lou sat at the dining room table, the chair pushed far back to give his long legs plenty of room. He was wearing tight, faded jeans and a black tee-shirt. With his long dark hair, he looked more like the front man of a heavy metal band than a ghost hunter.

"You came over just to check on me?" I handed Lou his tea and settled into the chair adjacent to his.

"Yes. Whatever my feelings may have been about Maxwell, I know you cared a lot for him. Daisy said you were actually there when it happened."

I nodded. "The hunter shot his arrow and Maxwell just…" I waved my hands, like a magician making a rabbit vanish.

"An arrow seems like an archaic choice." Lou spoke offhandedly, as if Maxwell's banishing was a scholarly matter.

"How else would they do it? Apparently the arrow has to be dipped in holy water and blessed by a priest."

"You could easily do the same with a bullet or a knife." Lou's voice dropped and he seemed to be speaking to himself. "Of course, anyone nearby would hear the gunshot if you used a bullet. A knife means you'd have to actually get up close to the demon. I guess an arrow does make sense."

"Thanks for clarifying." I couldn't keep the sarcastic edge out of my voice. "The hunter failed to explain his weapon choice when I ran into him on Monday."

Lou's eyebrows shot up. "Did he come after you, too?"

"Nah. We ran into each other at the cathedral. I'm sure he could understand why I wasn't thrilled to see him. He wasn't mean to me. In fact, I think he meant to be helpful, like you have been."

Actually, I realized, there were a few similarities between Lou's advice and the hunter's.

"I guess now I don't need that St. Michael medallion you gave me," I said.

Lou's eyes narrowed. "I think you should keep it."

I pulled the chain from underneath my shirt in answer. I had put it back on when I went to work Tuesday morning and hadn't taken it off since. Maxwell had proven to me that demons were real, so I wasn't going to take any chances. I doubted that if I ever met another one, he'd be as concerned for my welfare as Maxwell had been. He would also probably not be as handsome, or as charming, or as good in bed, but then, I doubted anyone—demon or human—ever would be.

Lou smiled, satisfied, and he rose. "Well, I'd better get home. I am sorry you've had to go through this, Boo."

"Thanks, Lou." I stood on my toes so I could wrap my arms around him in a hug. "And thanks for stopping by."

No sooner had Lou walked out the door than Daisy called. Her voice was excited and nervous. "I think we have a case," she said. "I want to go meet the family tomorrow, and I want the whole team to go with me."

"Just for an introductory meeting?"

"Yes. This family has a ghost that seems really agitated."

"Is the ghost attacking a family member?"

"No. It's upset about someone named Betty."

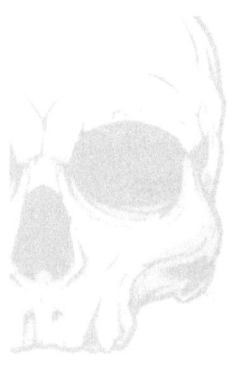

THIRTEEN

I bounced nervously as I sat at a traffic light Thursday afternoon. I was meeting the rest of The Seekers at the address Daisy had provided. The family had wanted to meet early, before dinner, which meant I had to drive straight there from work.

Daisy had refused to divulge more details on the phone, saying she preferred me to hear it firsthand from the family so none of the details got mixed up. I had been anxious all day. The fact that the ghost was upset about someone with the same name as me was probably just a coincidence, but it still bothered me. I hoped that I would meet the family and find out that the ghost was referring to a former resident of the house or a friend of the family's.

I pulled up in front of a pretty townhouse just two streets over from Maxwell's. This street wasn't as quaint— the cobblestones had long ago been replaced with asphalt —but it was still pretty and was clearly a nicer section of the Victorian district.

Daisy and Shaun got out of their car when they saw me. Shaun squeezed my shoulder and just said, "Sorry, Boo." Daisy, of course, caught me up in a hug and wanted to know how I was doing. I assured her that I'd feel a lot better once this meeting was over.

Shaun spotted Lou's truck turning onto the street, and we waited for him to join us so we could walk together up the stairs of the townhouse.

"This looks a lot like Maxwell's house," Shaun said casually as he rang the doorbell. "Oh, sorry, Betty."

"It's okay. It's not like we can't ever talk about him. He might be gone, but I don't want to forget him."

The door opened, and I straightened my shoulders and forced a smile onto my face.

"I'm Carla Jensen," the woman standing there said, patting her short brown hair self-consciously. Carla had probably been really pretty when she was younger.

She waved us all inside, and it wasn't until we were seated in a very modern living room that Daisy introduced all of us by name. When she motioned to me and said, "This is our founder, Betty Boorman," Carla stared at me with open curiosity.

It took everything I had to keep that smile on my face.

As we spoke, first one, and then another young boy thumped down the stairs and raced into the living room. They looked to be about five and seven, and I instantly noticed that they had inherited their mother's curious stare.

"Are they…" I began, letting my question trail off when Carla instantly nodded.

"Oh, yes, they know all about Faith."

"Faith?"

"Sure. She's the ghost who haunts this house." Carla spoke casually, taking the usual Savannah approach to having a resident ghost: as long as it's not a troublemaker, a ghost is welcome to join the family.

"How did you come to call her Faith?" Daisy asked.

"It's her name. She told me," the oldest boy spoke up. He was sitting on the armrest of the chair Carla occupied, and she reached up to pat him fondly. "Tell your story, Bryan."

"When I was little, she liked to play with my blocks. They had letters on them, and I would spell out words. I asked her to spell out her name, and she did."

"You saw her move the blocks?" I asked.

"No. She wouldn't do that kind of stuff in front of me. I left, and when I came back, the blocks said 'Faith.'"

"That's a very impressive story," Daisy said. I knew she wasn't just patronizing the boy. If he indeed had communicated with a ghost and had convinced it to manipulate objects, then he deserved praise for the feat.

"Faith was already here when we moved in," Carla took up the story. "We'd hear footsteps in the bedrooms when we were all downstairs, and objects would get moved around. Then, of course, Bryan started to see her. We thought at first it was just an imaginary friend, but when Derek, our youngest, got older and started talking about her, too, we gave the story more credence."

"You indicated on the phone that things have changed recently," Daisy prompted.

"Yes, and not a gradual change, either. Overnight Faith went from a fairly typical ghost to," Carla stared over our heads, looking for the right words, "something out of a horror movie."

"There has been violence?" When I thought of horror movies, I thought of big trouble.

"No, no, not like that. It's more like she's really upset, and we don't know why. I feel like she's trying to tell us something, but we can't make sense of it. Faith has indicated the name Betty, but whether it's a message for or from someone by that name, or a warning about someone by that name, we just don't know."

Carla continued when she saw the anxious looks on all of our faces. "Faith's footsteps got louder, like she was stomping down the upstairs hall or even jumping up and down. It was almost like a child having a temper tantrum. More objects started being moved, not just from one shelf to another, but into dangerous spots. A vase wound up on the staircase Monday morning, and Scott didn't see it because he never turns the hall light on when he goes to make coffee. He knocked the vase down the stairs and it shattered, but he could just as easily have tripped over it and fallen.

"That was the first thing that happened. It just got worse, and on Monday night, she kept all of us from sleeping with her noise. The worst so far happened when we woke up Wednesday morning."

Carla stopped and looked pointedly at me.

"What happened on Wednesday morning?" I prompted.

"I woke up to Derek screaming and crying. I ran into his room and there were words written in blood all over his wall."

Well, that was creepy.

"That's when we knew we needed help," a man's voice broke in. "I'm Scott. Sorry I wasn't here earlier; I had to work a little late." Scott leaned down and kissed Carla on the top of the head before turning his attention back to us. "We looked online for paranormal investigators, but we weren't sure who to contact. We found the website for The Savannah Spirit Seekers, and, well, it just seemed like too much of a coincidence that there was a girl named Betty on the team."

"You said you think the ghost's message has to do with that name. How do you know?" I asked.

Carla and Scott exchanged glances. "She spelled out the name," Scott finally said.

"Do you know whether a Betty has ever lived in this house?" Carla and Scott both shook their heads. "Perhaps you have a family member with that name?" Again, they answered in the negative.

I turned to the boys. "Do either of you have a friend at school named Betty, or has Faith ever mentioned having a friend by that name?"

They answered in unison with a firm, "Nope."

Well, darn. I was out of options on that line of questioning. Still, I knew I'd be at the Historical Society doing research soon enough. Just because the family didn't know about a former resident with my name, didn't mean she hadn't existed.

"Do you want to see the wall?" Scott asked.

"I'm surprised you didn't clean it up already," Shaun said.

"We wanted to leave it there long enough for you to look at. I'm going to clean it up and repaint it tomorrow."

We trooped upstairs, the boys leading the way proudly, pointing out places where they'd seen or heard Faith along the way. It was like our own little ghost tour.

Actually seeing the wall was far worse than anything I could have imagined. I was the last one to enter Derek's room, but everyone was pressed against the far wall so I had a clear view of the ghost's message.

The entire wall was covered in a big, childish scrawl. "Betty, Betty, Betty," the letters spelled, over and over, line after line of my name. The red letters had dripped to look almost comically nightmarish.

I felt faint. The letters began to tilt, and I shut my eyes against the wave of dizziness, instinctively stretching out my hand. Lou caught it and lowered me into a low chair. He sank down onto one knee and peered at me. "Are you all right?"

"I wasn't prepared to see that." I opened my eyes but kept them focused on the carpet. I didn't want to look at the wall again, afraid I really would faint if I did. "I figured the ghost had just spelled my name using blocks again."

"It's not blood, at least. You can feel better about that, Boo." Shaun sounded smug: there was nothing he loved better than debunking something. "Carla, Scott, look: there was a container of red paint behind the dresser. It's empty."

"From Bryan's art kit," Carla said, embarrassed. "I can't believe we jumped right to the blood theory."

Scott seemed almost angry. "Boys, I want you to be honest. Did one of you do this as a joke?"

They had answered me with a "nope," but their dad received a somber, "No, sir."

"I doubt they would have been able to reach all the way to the ceiling, anyway," Daisy pointed out. "Repetition like this is typical when a spirit is trying to communicate something. It's like it becomes obsessed with trying to be understood. You see it in EVP sessions, automatic writing, even psychics will report getting the same message repeated, like a tape recorder on a loop."

"Then what should we do?" Carla asked.

I spoke up then, though I was addressing the floor. "We'll come hold an investigation here as soon as possible. If Faith can't get her message across in writing, maybe she can tell us or show us. We'll try as many communication methods as we can. In the meantime, whenever Faith starts acting up, assure her that you know she has a message. Tell her we're coming back soon, and we want to help her."

"What does your schedule look like for this weekend?" Daisy asked Carla.

"I think we should check our calendars downstairs," Lou said quietly. I saw him gesture at me out of the corner of my eye before he reached down and took my hand to help me up. I didn't raise my head until we were in the hallway.

The Jensens had something planned for Friday, so we agreed to come over on Saturday to investigate. That meant I would have time beforehand to do some research.

Shaun, Daisy, and Lou huddled around me once we got outside. They each asked me some variation of "Are you okay?" I nodded. "That wall was really spooky. Whomever the ghost is referring to, I didn't like seeing my own name like that. Add to it that I've had pretty much the worst week ever, and it just got to be too much. At least Mr. Jensen will have painted over it before we come back on Saturday."

"And hopefully by then you'll be better rested," Lou said. "You look tired. Are you having nightmares about the hunter?"

"How did you guess? I have the same dream every night. He's shooting an arrow, and I'm screaming." Lou shrugged. "It was a traumatic experience for you. It makes sense you'd dream about it."

I was the last one to get in my car. I stood and watched as Lou pulled away, wondering how he'd known about my recurring dream.

———⁂———

I didn't want to get out of bed on Saturday morning. I woke up to the realization that it had been one week since Maxwell had been banished. There was a lot of research to cram into my day, though. I could do a little bit of research from home, so I looked over the few historical records that the city has online while I sipped my coffee. Mina sat on my lap, purring happily while I worked.

When I typed in the house's address, I got the basics: it had been built in 1876 by Jeremiah Stone. It wasn't much, but it did, at least, give me a name and a year with which to begin my search.

The Georgia Historical Society was practically deserted. The records section was usually quiet, but for most of the afternoon the only people in there were the sole employee and me.

Which is why, when I looked at the house's records, she was the only person to hear me shout.

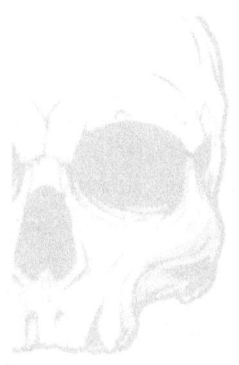

FOURTEEN

I hadn't expected to find anyone with my name in the list of the townhouse's records since ownership was usually in a man's name. Still, looking at the list helped me know which surnames to look for when I started going through other records.

It was the house's second owner that had caused my outburst. In 1891, the original owner had sold his home to a man named Maxwell Damon.

No, I corrected myself. Not a man. A demon.

The Maxwell I knew had been gone for a week, but his Victorian persona had jumped right out of the nineteenth century and into my investigation. After my initial surprise, I actually laughed. It seemed like something Maxwell would have contrived, had he still been alive to do it. He would have found a lot of humor in injecting himself into yet another ghost story.

Wondering about Maxwell's possible involvement in the story of either Faith or this unidentified Betty was sobering. I knew Maxwell had been responsible for a number of deaths, as well as some lingering ghosts. Had he been involved in Faith's death?

I started my newspaper search with 1891, when Maxwell had taken up residence in the townhouse. He sold the home in 1896, a surprisingly short time after moving in. That five-year span took up much of my afternoon but yielded nothing.

I went back to the beginning, searching the records from the time of the house's construction in 1876. I had some luck when I got to 1879: the obituaries included a listing for a child, age six, named Sarah Faith Stone. She had died of the measles.

Now that Faith had been identified, that left me with a couple of hours to track down the mysterious Betty.

I found nothing.

The only person who left the building after me was an employee, who shooed me out the door so he could lock up behind me. I sighed and walked home slowly, realizing there was a good reason so few people had been indoors with me. It was a perfectly beautiful day. The sun was out, and it was warm in the sunshine but comfortably cool in the shade of the trees in the squares. The downside to being a ghost hunter is that you're usually asleep during the beautiful Saturdays or stuck doing research, like me.

I decided that coming across Maxwell's name during my search today was far better than the sunshine. It had felt really good to see that familiar name on the page.

Instead of going inside my apartment, I headed straight for my car. I drove to Fort Pulaski, stopping at a florist's on the way. I chose a bouquet of lilies. When I got to the fort, I tried to walk down toward the moat without calling attention to myself. It's hard to be inconspicuous when you're carrying flowers at a tourist attraction.

Maybe people would think I was leaving them for a relative who had died there during the war.

I didn't want to leave the flowers in the middle of the grass where Maxwell had actually been banished. They'd be picked up and thrown away by a grounds worker in no time if I left them out in the open like that. Instead, I walked out toward the marsh. There, where the reeds began to choke out the grass, I nestled the bouquet down where they wouldn't be easily spotted.

"I miss you, Maxwell," I said quietly. "I love you."

Before I could start crying again—really, hadn't I done enough of that in the past week?—I turned and walked away. A few children stared at me curiously, but everyone else was oblivious to the private funeral I had just conducted.

I napped for an hour when I got home, but even in the daylight, my nightmare found me once I was asleep. I awoke with a start, my lungs filling with air to unleash another scream. This time, my nightmare had changed slightly: the raindrops falling around me were bright red drops of blood.

———

I was the first to arrive at the Jensens' that night. Carla answered the front door and ushered me inside, asking eagerly when the rest of the team would arrive. I assured her they would be along shortly, but she was so anxious that she immediately launched into a description of the latest activity.

"Faith has been acting up just as much," Carla began, pointing me to the same chair I had occupied before. "We tried doing what you said, telling her we knew she had something to say. Every time one of us said, 'They will be here Saturday to talk to you,' she would quiet down. I think she understood us."

"That's encouraging. If she is aware that we're here to help and she's that eager to communicate, then maybe we'll get some answers tonight."

"But there's more! We told her that we knew she wanted our attention and to please stop moving objects to places where we could get hurt. We promised her she didn't need to do things like that to get our attention."

"Did it work?"

"So far. She's still stomping up and down on the second floor, and things are still getting moved, but we haven't had any more close calls. Now things are moving from one side of Derek's desk to the other, or from the mantle to the hall table. The usual stuff, but definitely more often than usual."

"I think you'll be excited to know what I learned while researching your house." I was about to continue when the doorbell rang. Carla excused herself and while she was gone, her youngest son came into the room.

"You're Derek, right?" I asked.

"Yes. And you're Betty."

"That's right. You remembered."

"No, she told me."

"I'm not surprised that your mom told you about my name. Me having the same name as the person Faith is talking about is what we call a coincidence."

"That's not what I mean."

"What do you mean?"

Carla entered at that moment, leading Lou, Shaun, and Daisy. Lou and Shaun were lugging our video cameras and monitor, and Carla was busy directing them. "The kitchen is down the hall, the third door on your right. Daisy, make yourself at home; Betty is already here. Derek, what did I tell you? You get back upstairs right now."

I started to protest, but Derek was already walking away, and I didn't want to contradict his mother's orders. Whatever he had been trying to say, his message was as cryptic as Faith's.

Daisy and I pitched in to set up our base in the kitchen, but we decided to wait until we'd talked with Carla and Scott before we placed the cameras. Carla shouted up the stairs for Scott to come down, and he was wearing paint-spattered jeans when he joined us.

"There may still be some wet paint up there," he warned us.

"I'm just glad you got that writing covered up." I felt a chill just remembering the sight of my name all over that wall. "On a happier note, I did find some interesting information while researching your house."

Everyone quieted to listen to me; I hadn't even filled in the other Seekers about what I'd learned.

I told them about Faith's obituary, pulling a copy out of my case so the Jensen family could have it. I knew their boys would be excited to see something about Faith in a newspaper, even if it was her death announcement.

Carla and Scott were impressed, and they were satisfied to know that their eldest son's pronouncement about Faith's name had been correct.

I added a few more details about the house's history, but I was really speaking to my team when I said, "And the second owner purchased the house in 1891. His name was Maxwell Damon."

Daisy gasped. Lou frowned. Shaun's was the only audible response, shouting, "No way!"

"Is that significant?" Scott asked. "I've never heard of him."

Shaun quickly covered for me. "His name came up in another investigation we did. Savannah was a lot smaller then, so it's inevitable that some of the same people are going to crop up during case research." Shaun turned and gave me a quick wink before raising his eyebrows. His face clearly said, "I want to know all about this later."

Carla filled the rest of the team in on the continued activity. She and Scott were going to take their boys to Scott's parents for the night, and they promised to return by midnight. Carla hinted that she wanted to see us in action, which was fine by me.

Their sons trooped downstairs with their overnight backpacks, and on their way out the door, Carla suddenly stopped and turned to me. "Did you find anyone named Betty in your research?"

"No, but that doesn't mean no one by that name ever lived here. I'd have to research family trees, and even then, it's possible the Betty being referred to was a household servant, or a nanny, or even just a family friend. We'll have to ask Faith tonight if she can tell us."

"Good luck. Our cell numbers are on the kitchen counter if you need anything at all."

With the house to ourselves, we quickly got one camera set up in Derek's room and another pointed down the upstairs hallway. Daisy and Shaun were going to sit in Derek's room first for an EVP session. "It's a little weird to be on an investigation without Carter," she said, shoving her tape recorder into a pocket. "We've worked with him a lot lately."

"Yes, I miss him terribly," I said, mockingly putting a hand to my forehead. "Oh, Daze, I totally forgot to ask you what's going on with that job at his dad's firm. I'm sorry. I just got distracted."

"Don't apologize. I haven't heard back, other than a phone call from Mr. Lansford's secretary."

"And?" I knew Daisy had something good to report by the look on her face.

"I have an interview on Tuesday, at eleven o'clock."

I clapped my hands. "Daisy, congratulations! That's great!"

My week might have been a bad one, but at least Daisy had good news to share. I still didn't quite trust Carter, but I was happy that she had an interview with such a prestigious law firm.

Daisy and Shaun headed upstairs while I settled in at the folding table we'd set up in the kitchen. Lou was already seated there, his eyes on the split-screen monitor that showed both camera feeds. He already had a pen in his hand, ready to jot down any anomalies in his notebook.

I yawned as soon as I sat down. "Sorry," I said. "I took a nap today, but I don't feel at all rested. That stupid nightmare again."

Lou nodded knowingly. "It will fade in time. I brought the coffee maker. Help yourself."

I glanced behind me at the kitchen counter and saw Lou's small coffee maker, already plugged in. We usually carry our own when we investigate homes; it's a lot easier, and more polite, if the family doesn't have to clean up after us.

Brewing coffee was the only interesting thing that happened for that first hour. Daisy and Shaun ended their EVP session and joined us in the kitchen.

"We asked her to spell out her message with that same set of blocks she used before," Shaun explained. "According to those kids, she won't do it if anyone is in the room with her."

And so we sat. The camera in Derek's room clearly showed the blocks, and my eyes began to hurt from squinting at the tiny blocks on the monitor.

They never moved.

"I think it's time for Lou and me to give it a shot," I said finally, rubbing my eyes. "It's either that or go blind sitting here."

Even though Scott had painted over the wall in Derek's room, I still entered with some trepidation. Everything was as it should be, though, and I was disappointed that Faith hadn't moved the blocks for us.

"We'll keep this brief," I told Lou as we sat cross-legged

on the floor to do an EVP session. He put his tape recorder on the carpet between us and motioned to me to begin.

"Hello, Faith. My name is Betty. Isn't that a funny coincidence?" I went on, urging Faith to come and talk to us. I asked her what she was trying to tell us and who Betty was.

The worst thing about EVP sessions is that you don't know if you're actually getting results until later. Sometimes I will sit there for ages and wind up with nothing. Other times, I will get frustrated and give up, only to listen to the recording later and hear responses.

So far, though, Faith seemed to be a ghost who preferred to show, not say. After twenty minutes of talking, I turned off the tape recorder and repeated Daisy and Shaun's request to communicate with the blocks. To show Faith what I meant, I spelled out my name with them.

I noticed drawing paper on a table in the corner, so I took several sheets and put them down on the floor along with a couple of markers. "Faith, you can also use this paper to write on. We really want to know your message for us."

"Daisy, can you see the paper?" I asked into my radio.

"Just tilt it up to the right a bit."

With everything in place, Lou and I returned to the kitchen for another round of staring at the monitor.

We were still sitting there when Carla and Scott Jensen returned home. "This doesn't look as exciting as I'd pictured it," Scott said.

"We were hoping she would move the blocks or write on the paper," I explained, sliding back so they could see the monitor. "Nothing yet."

"Betty, why don't you and I take Carla up there for an EVP session? Maybe Faith will be responsive if it's just us girls," Daisy suggested.

Carla quickly agreed after we explained to her what an EVP session was. Hopefully, with a member of the family there, Faith would feel comfortable enough to communicate. It was entirely possible that she was feeling shy around us because we were strangers.

Daisy led the way into Derek's bedroom, and she uttered a quick, "Oh!"

Carla stopped in the doorway. "Look what she's done."

I peeked over her shoulder and followed the beam of Daisy's flashlight.

Faith had found the markers, but she hadn't used them on the paper. She had written all over everything else.

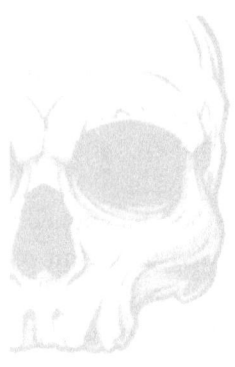

FIFTEEN

Faith had been careful to write on surfaces that weren't in the camera's view, and it was clear that she had been very busy. I didn't know what to say. Part of me wanted to scream, but another part of me wanted to apologize profusely to Carla for the mess she and Scott were now faced with cleaning.

Faith had written my name on the wall above Derek's bed, though this time she'd used a black marker, and the letters were only several inches tall. There was a tight block of "Betty Betty Betty" the width of the headboard.

The blue wooden headboard had "Yes Yes Yes" scrawled across it. The desk was untouched, but the seat of the chair blared "Live Live Live."

Those three words were repeated everywhere: on the closet doors, on the other walls, on the framed picture of Derek fishing with his dad, on the soccer jersey hanging from a hook on the back of the bedroom door.

The first words out of my mouth weren't the most eloquent. "Oh, hell."

"I don't understand," Carla said. Her voice was quiet but it began to rise to a near-hysterical pitch. "Why would she do this? What would make her so upset? What did you do to her?"

"And what do these words even mean?" The voice of

reason came from Daisy. "'Betty, Yes, Live'?" I heard a click and she spoke into her radio. "You three need to come up here, right now."

Lou, Shaun, and Scott were appropriately shocked when they saw the room, though they handled it with less emotion. "She's very clever," Lou said. "She must have used markers that were on the desk, where we couldn't see her taking them."

I didn't realize that Daisy had moved to stand next to me until she wrapped her arm around me. "It's you," she whispered. She didn't sound scared, just matter of fact. Daisy's intuition had kicked into high gear, and she spoke with no hesitation. "Faith wants us to know the Betty she's been referring to is you. That's why she added 'Yes' and 'Live.' You're alive, and she's talking about you rather than someone who's already dead."

"But why?"

"Let's find out." Daisy turned to Carla and Scott. "I'm so sorry about this mess. Clearly, whatever Faith wants to communicate is very important to her. We'd like to see if she'll tell us more tonight."

"Where's she going to write it? On the ceiling?" Carla had tears in her eyes.

Scott looked as curious as I felt, but one glance at his wife made up his mind. "I think we'd better call it a night."

I knew we all looked disappointed. Faith had finally begun to communicate, and we had to give up just when her message was getting even more mysterious.

"She never acted like this until you came here." Carla's voice was low.

I opened my mouth to say that, in fact, Faith *had* acted like this before we came. After all, it was her writing on the wall that had prompted the Jensen family to call us in the first place. One look at Carla's face silenced me, though.

"We're very sorry," Shaun said. "We only asked her if

she'd like to tell us something. This behavior is highly unusual, even for an agitated spirit. After we've gone, please encourage her to tell you what is so important. Otherwise, I fear the activity here won't stop."

"Please go."

Carla didn't have to tell me twice. I hated that she blamed this on us, but I knew that I'd be upset, too, if I were in her situation. We could go home and not have to deal with the case anymore. Carla, on the other hand, would have to explain to her youngest son why half of his things were ruined.

We filed downstairs quietly. I felt like I was a kid again, being sent to my room for doing something wrong. I knew I shouldn't feel ashamed, and yet I did.

This isn't our fault, I told myself firmly. Even if the ghost is talking about me.

We packed up quickly and quietly. We were about to head out the door when Scott joined us. Carla had stayed upstairs, and Shaun apologized to Scott for upsetting her.

"It's not your fault," Scott said. It felt good to hear that. "She's just in shock. If it were up to me, we'd all be down here watching your camera feed. I think you're right: Faith isn't going to calm down until she's convinced that she's gotten her message through. I'll call you if—when—something else happens."

"Thank you." Shaun extended his hand to Scott. "We appreciate you calling us. If anything turns up on our tape recorders, we'll let you know. And we are very sorry for upsetting your wife."

"Not your fault," Scott repeated.

I was the last out the door, and Scott held me back with a gentle hand on my arm. "Betty, a moment, please?"

I stopped in the open doorway, my case hanging from one shoulder.

"Why would Faith be trying to get a message to you?"

"I don't know. How she could even know who I am is a mystery."

"Maybe another ghost is trying to contact you through her? That does happen sometimes, right?"

"It's possible, and it's something I've considered. I just can't think of anything a ghost might have to say to me. Faith seems to be having trouble articulating her message. If she's passing along information secondhand, maybe she only got some of the details. I'll take a look at past cases we've done and see if anything stands out. I can call former clients and ask if activity has increased for them lately."

Scott nodded. "I think that's a good idea. Is there anyone else you can ask?"

I thought for a moment. "A lot of ghosts are tied to a location, like the place they died or somewhere they lived for many years. I don't think ghosts exactly meet up for coffee to share the latest gossip. However, I'll check with a reliable contact I know who might be able to help."

"Another ghost hunter?"

"Ah, no. Lieutenant Griffin is a ghost. But he's very aware and might be able to tell me if there's some..." I laced my fingers together, trying to think of the right term, "paranormal network."

Scott smiled wanly. "You do lead an interesting life."

"Yes. And please, even though what Faith did tonight is a little out of line, please don't be mad at her. She's just frustrated and communicating the only way she knows how."

"You mean I can't ground her for two weeks?"

"You could try, but I doubt it would work." I smiled politely and shook Scott's hand, and he thanked me again for our work. I left feeling frustrated and confused. I also felt guilty about Derek's room and Carla's reaction to it, even though, as I'd already told myself a dozen times, it wasn't our fault.

I decided to speak to Lieutenant Griffin as soon as I got home. It was one in the morning, but I was wide awake.

"Lieutenant, I have some questions you might be able to answer for me. If you can, rattle the window blinds once for yes and twice for no. Do you understand?"

My living room blinds gave one firm bang.

"The ghost we met tonight seems to know who I am, and we think she might have a message for me from another ghost. Do ghosts talk to each other?"

My blinds clattered again, but it was hesitant this time.

"Not very often, then," I guessed. I received an affirmative answer.

"Most ghosts seem tied to their locations. Do some travel?"

Another hesitant yes.

"Are there other ways for ghosts to communicate?"

This time, the answer was a very strong yes.

I stopped and thought. It was difficult trying to discern the truth using only yes and no questions. My instinct was to ask, "How?" but that would get me nowhere. Unless, of course, I could learn Morse code and have Lieutenant Griffin tap his answer out on my blinds.

Actually, that wasn't a bad idea. I'd have to look into that.

For now, though, we had to stick to the basics. "Can spirits who have already crossed over come back and spread news among ghosts?"

Lieutenant Griffin told me that they couldn't.

"Maybe ghosts spread news they hear from people coming in and out of the places they haunt?"

No.

"What, are ghosts just psychic and able to bounce their thoughts from place to place?"

Lieutenant Griffin gave his most forceful affirmation yet.

"Really? I had no idea." I had never suspected that ghosts could communicate with each other telepathically. Maybe that was how mediums came by their abilities: they somehow tap into that network to "hear" conversations among ghosts.

"Thanks, Lieutenant. This case has me frustrated, but you've been a big help. If you ever hear news about me from other ghosts, can you please let me know?"

There was a final tap against my blinds, and our conversation was over. Knowing that ghosts could relay messages to each other certainly gave me a lot to think about. The biggest questions I had were, of course, which ghost had been talking to Faith about me, and why?

I wrote those two questions in my notebook on Sunday morning. As I went through paperwork from past cases, I asked, "Why do you want to talk to me?" out loud for each ghost I had ever encountered.

By the time I'd exhausted my list, two cases stood out as potential reasons for Faith's urgent need to communicate with me. One had been a male ghost haunting a home on Tybee Island. He'd been a persistent flirt, constantly touching my hair and tugging at the back of my shirt. No one else in our group had gotten such treatment, and the family reported that he was ordinarily a docile ghost. They had just wanted to get some answers as to who he might have been in life, and why he was still hanging around. My research had turned up the death of a young man who'd lived there with his family. He had been killed in a car accident.

The second case that seemed a likely option was one of

our more recent ones: Jasper Whitney had haunted his former law firm in the Everett-Tattnall House, and he had warned me of danger during our investigation there. Jasper was well aware of who I was, he knew me by name, and it was possible he had more to say to me.

I hoped one of those two cases would hold some answers for me. Satisfied for the time being, I closed my notebook and stood. As I rose, I heard a soft pop behind me.

I turned and found myself inches away from a man I'd never seen in my life.

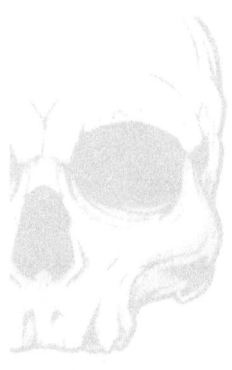

SIXTEEN

I had recognized that popping sound as a sign that a demon had materialized in my dining room, where I'd been working. My first, brief thought was that Maxwell had come over for a visit. My second, more disquieting thought was that Maxwell had been banished to hell and would never materialize in my apartment again.

So who, then, was this demon currently engaged in a staring contest with me?

He was short and had olive skin. His eyes and hair were dark brown, and he was one of the most perfectly ordinary people I'd ever seen. I briefly wondered if demons got to choose their physical appearance when they came to Earth in human form. Why choose to be so bland when you could be drop-dead gorgeous?

"Who are you?" I asked.

"Now, Betty, that's no way to greet someone who has been of such help to you."

I instantly recognized the slight accent. "Tage."

"Very good."

"Why are you here?" The demon still had his eyes locked on mine, and he was close enough that I could have reached out and hugged him.

"Honestly, such a lack of manners. I'm in your home. Shouldn't you be offering me a sweet tea or something? I thought you Southern girls were all hospitality and kindness. I'm sure you never treated Maxwell like this."

"Maxwell was always welcome in my home."

"You're implying that I am not."

"You're an intruder, as far as I'm concerned."

At those words, my window blinds began to bang urgently. Tage finally pulled his eyes from mine, and he looked startled at the sudden activity.

"It's okay, Lieutenant," I said. "For now." I turned my attention to Tage again, taking advantage of the distraction to step away from him. "I assume you came here for a reason?"

"Of course."

"Then you may as well sit down. I'm all out of sweet tea, though." I knew I was being rude, and it was probably the last thing I should be doing. After all, Tage had helped guide me through the aftermath of Maxwell's banishment, so I should have been thanking him. He was also a demon, and it was just never a good idea to get on a demon's bad side.

Darn, the guilt was setting in. Tage had been right about us Southern girls. I had a slightly kinder tone of voice when I added, "But I do have Coke, or I can make another pot of coffee."

"That's more like it, but I'll pass, thank you." Tage sat down on my couch, and I had a chance to observe him more closely as I joined him, settling as far from him as I could without sitting on the armrest. He was dressed casually in jeans and a tee-shirt from a rock concert. I was struck again with how ordinary he was. He was the kind of guy you could pass on the street without ever noticing.

Maybe that was the point. Maxwell had favored a flashy approach to being a demon, but Tage must prefer subtlety. That could be dangerous. I would have to watch myself with this demon.

Before I could ask my own questions, Tage jumped in with, "How are you getting along since Maxwell's demise?"

"Okay. I miss him a lot, but it's only been a week."

"How bad are the nightmares?"

First Lou, and now Tage. Was somebody spying on my subconscious? I shrugged, trying to downplay their intensity. "I understand it's typical to have them after a traumatic event."

Tage gave a short laugh. "It's typical to have them after witnessing a banishing. They cause a lot of young hunters to turn to less disturbing lines of work. You think yours are bad, but they're even worse for the one whose hand fitted the arrow to the bow."

"That actually makes me feel a little better. If he's having nightmares, then I'm perfectly okay with that. I know the hunter felt it was his duty to banish Maxwell, but no one asked me how I felt about it."

"No, they rarely consider anyone's opinion but their own and their priest's."

"What brings you here, Tage?"

"I'm here to help you, Betty."

I raised my eyebrows.

"I already helped you once. You know I would not lead you astray."

"I wasn't aware that I needed any help."

Tage leaned over and put his hand on my knee. I could feel his warmth through my slacks. I closed my eyes briefly, remembering the only other man whose skin radiated heat that way.

"You need my help to get Maxwell back," Tage said.

"That's impossible. He's gone." If there had been a way, I would have tried it. Was Tage here to tease me, to make me feel Maxwell's loss even more? It would be a typically demonic thing to do: make me feel as much despair as possible so I'd lose all hope and faith.

"There is a way."

"There's not. He's been banished and there's nothing anyone can do about it. I won't let you do this to me."

"You say there's not, but I say you know very little of demons. You dated one for, what, a month? You are far from an expert on our ways."

I remained silent. I wasn't going to let Tage draw me into a false hope.

"There is a way, Betty, and you're the only one who can do it. I can't."

I frowned. "Clearly you're not going to leave until you've had your say. Get it over with."

"Of all the people on this earth, no one loved Maxwell the way you did. There is no living soul who feels as deeply for him as you do, no one else who would be willing to do whatever it takes to save him from the torment of hell."

I nodded. Tage was probably right about that. Maxwell drew plenty of looks from other women, but their interest was superficial.

"He's suffering, Betty. Right now, the man you love is engulfed in flames that scorch and sear but do not consume. For him, it is unending torture. Even his memories of you will slip away as the agony becomes the only thing he knows."

Tage was saying the truth I had been so ardently avoiding. I had seen a glimpse of hell, and I knew what Maxwell suffered now, but I had blocked it from my mind. Knowing Maxwell was gone from this life was bad enough, but thinking of the life to which he had returned was worse. I felt guilty that I was trying to move on with my own life: going on an investigation, going to work, and seeing my friends while Maxwell was in hell.

"Betty, you can bring him back from that. You can give him his life back. How can you not do everything in your power to save him? He's saved your life on more than one occasion. This is the least you can do."

"What do I have to do?" I asked.

"All you have to do is offer up an exchange."

"An exchange of lives, you mean." My tone was flat. Of course there would be no easy solution from a demon.

"Certainly not. Hell doesn't want your life. Just your soul."

I shrank back on the couch, horrified at Tage's words.

"It's an easy choice, Betty: go through the remainder of your long life, knowing all the while that the one you love is in never-ending torment, or free him. All it takes is your soul."

I shook my head. "But then I'd be the one going through that torment. How is that fair?"

"It's not about being fair. It's about doing what's right. You tried to be rude to me when I arrived, yet here I am, sitting on your couch like we're old friends. You're too good to allow Maxwell's suffering to continue. You're too good to forget your own kindness."

"No. No way. I can't do something like that."

"I'd do it if I had a soul to trade," Tage said quietly. "Maxwell has saved me many times over the years, and he's always been a good friend. If I was the only one who could bring him back, I would."

I was silent. Tage stood and offered a hand to help me up. I put my hand in his before I considered what I was doing. His grasp was firm but gentle as he pulled me to my feet.

"You don't have to make up your mind now. Take some time and consider your choice." Tage's hand was still holding onto mine, and he gripped my fingers firmly, sending a wave of heat up my arm. "I'm not trying to cause extra grief, Betty. I truly want to help Maxwell, and I know you do, too. You're the only one who can help him."

Tage dropped my hand and stepped back, but I had one last question. "If I agree to it, what happens?"

"You sign a contract stating that you waive your right to judgment, and your soul will pass into hell at the end of your natural life." Tage's lips curled up in a hint of a smile. "I'll be in touch." There was another "pop," and Tage disappeared.

I buried my face in my hands. "God help me," I mumbled. I had never meant the phrase so literally in my life. What was I supposed to do? Of course I wanted to help Maxwell, but trading my soul so that he could continue his demonic destruction here on Earth didn't seem like the right thing to do. On the other hand, he hadn't been so destructive since we'd started dating. Plus, wasn't I supposed to adhere to that whole "turn the other cheek," Golden Rule stuff? Trading my soul for another's survival seemed like the morally correct thing to do, even if that other person was actually a demon.

Clearly, I had a lot of things to think about.

I was pretty useless for the rest of the day. No matter what I tried to do—watch a movie, clean the apartment, take a walk—all I could think about was Tage's proposal. I wondered if a signed contract could really be binding. I'd always thought that the idea of signing a contract with the Devil was just a legend, and it was almost comical that it was true. It seemed so silly and archaic. If only I had a good lawyer, I thought, I could sign the contract and then sue to get out of my obligation. Betty Boorman versus hell.

Sunday night brought little sleep, and when I did sleep, my nightmare was back in full force. Its intensity had yet to fade. I always fill a travel mug with coffee before I leave for work, and usually it gets me through my morning office routine of checking e-mail, organizing my day's to-do list, and listening to the receptionist tell me the latest gossip.

This morning, though, I took the last sip as I was pulling into the parking lot of Coastal Health Hospital.

I was nursing my third cup of coffee and staring bleary-eyed at some text for a newsletter that needed editing when a sudden thought struck me. If I sold my soul, then this might be as good as things would ever get for me. My only heaven would be what I had in this life, and it might never be more than ghost hunting and an office job.

That was a lousy trade-off.

I ought to make the most of this life, anyway, regardless of what the afterlife might bring. I grabbed a sticky note and wrote "Get Awesome Life" in big letters. I stuck it to my computer monitor. It was a start, at least.

My lunch hour began with two phone calls: one to the Ballard family on Tybee Island and one to Alec Thornburn, the only member of the Whitney, Thornburn and Stiles law firm who was neither dead nor in jail.

Sandra Ballard answered the phone immediately and was understandably surprised to hear my voice on the other end. She assured me that Rory, their resident ghost, had been quite quiet. "My oldest started college last month, and Rory seems to miss her a lot," Sandra explained. "She came home last weekend for a visit, and he followed her all over the house, tapping away on her shoulder. Otherwise, there haven't been any changes in his behavior."

Okay, Rory was a little lonely since one of his housemates was gone, but that didn't seem like something that would make anyone, let alone Faith, so very upset.

Mr. Thornburn, his receptionist informed me, was in court and wouldn't return to the firm until the next day. I sure hoped he'd have some insight into Faith's behavior.

My cell phone rang promptly at eight o'clock on Tuesday morning. I had just slid behind my desk, and I instinctively knew it was Alec Thornburn. I could hear his smile through the phone when I answered. "Betty, I was so pleased to see you had called. What can I do for you?"

"I was calling to check on Jasper." Jasper Whitney had been actively haunting the law firm since his death. His assistance in saving my life from the third partner in the firm had been the difference between me being shot and me, well, sitting here now talking to Mr. Thornburn.

"Jasper? Oh, he's quieted down quite a bit. Once we learned that he'd been murdered and Terrence got arrested, Jasper seemed satisfied. He still paces back and forth in his office, like he did when he was living, and Annabelle glimpses his shadow from the front desk now and then."

Darn it. Jasper had been my best bet for who might want to communicate with me. "Mr. Thornburn, I wonder if you'd do me a favor? Ask Jasper if he has a message for me."

"Do you think he has unfinished business with you?"

"Somebody does." I briefly told Mr. Thornburn about our current case, and my theory that Faith was trying to relay a message from another ghost.

Mr. Thornburn promised to check on Jasper for me, and I was again left wondering who might be looking for me.

My day took a turn for the better when Daisy called to say she'd been offered the job as a legal assistant to Mr. Lansford. She wanted me to join her and Shaun in an impromptu celebratory dinner.

That, of course, meant we headed for The Burglar Bar. It wasn't fancy, but it was our favorite place to meet up and had been the site for plenty of celebrations since we discovered the place while we were in college.

Shaun and Daisy had already snagged a table outside so we could enjoy the fall weather. Daisy jumped up out of her chair as I approached.

"Congratulations, Daze," I said, embracing her. "I'm really happy for you."

"Thanks. I'm so excited. I'm turning in my two-week notice at work tomorrow morning."

"How did you manage to get away for an interview?"

"I did it over my lunch hour. Then Mr. Lansford called in the middle of the afternoon to offer me the job, and I had to act casual so people around me wouldn't suspect. It was the hardest thing ever to not jump up and down."

Daisy related the details of her interview, adding that the job came with a significant raise. "And Mr. Lansford was polite, but I bet other lawyers hate facing him in court. He's got this presence." Daisy raised her arms and spread them wide. "You can feel the power."

"Poor Carter. Mr. Lansford must have been a scary father," Shaun observed.

"Speaking of Carter," Daisy said, "I'm going to have to do something nice for him. Get him a bottle of fancy wine or something as a thank you."

I laughed. "All this playing nice between you and Carter is just weird. I'm highly suspicious of you both."

"It got me a job."

"I can't argue with that."

We quieted down when our food arrived, and I saw Daisy looking at me keenly. "What is it?" she asked once our server walked away.

"I didn't realize I was being so obvious."

"Boo, it's me. I can tell something's wrong, but this isn't just sadness about Maxwell."

I glanced around to make sure none of the other diners

were paying attention to us and lowered my voice. I told Shaun and Daisy about my visit from Tage and his proposal. Shaun looked angry that Tage had even suggested such a thing, but Daisy's eyes filled with tears.

"Oh, poor Maxwell," she said as I finished.

"But Betty's not going to do it. It's just a trick by a demon who's trying to win her soul." Shaun looked at me pointedly.

"What if it could bring Maxwell back, though?" I asked.

Daisy shook her head. "Shaun's right. You can't possibly be considering this. He's a demon, Betty. He's back where he's supposed to be. I'm sorry. I know you don't want to hear it."

I nodded, but I was unconvinced. Refusing the deal was the smartest thing to do, but I still wasn't sure that it was the right thing. I started to say just that when Daisy's cell phone rang.

"Hang on," she said, fishing through her purse. She frowned at the caller ID. "Hello, Mrs. Strunk."

It took me a moment to realize with whom Daisy was speaking. Mrs. Strunk was the owner of Low Country Antiques, and even though the investigation hadn't been that long ago, so much had happened since then that I'd nearly forgotten about it.

Daisy's conversation wasn't long and mostly consisted of "Yes," "Really?" and "Oh, that's interesting." She eyed me the entire time, her eyes growing wider with each comment to Mrs. Strunk.

When Daisy finally hung up, her lips were pressed in a tight line of concern. "Mrs. Strunk's 'children' have been acting up," she began. "Instead of the laughter she usually hears, Mrs. Strunk has begun to hear words."

"How does that qualify as acting up?" Shaun asked.

"Because they are shouting at her." Daisy's eyes were still pinned on me.

"Okay, I'll bite. What are they shouting?"

"'Betty' and 'alive.'"

I shook my head. "What the hell is going on? We have already established that I'm alive. Why do ghosts keep having to remind me of that fact?"

"Maybe your life is in danger again. Perhaps they're trying to keep you alive," Shaun suggested.

"That doesn't make sense. If all this was happening back when we did the investigation at the Everett-Tattnall House, it would fit. But there's nothing dangerous going on right now. Lieutenant Griffin told me that ghosts can communicate telepathically, but Faith already made it clear that I'm the Betty she's talking about. Having Mrs. Strunk's kids telling me the same thing seems pointless."

"Maybe they don't realize that you got the same message from Faith." Daisy was stabbing her salad with her fork, murdering tomatoes as she thought. "They've established that it's you they're trying to reach. The next step is figuring out what they have to say to you."

"I don't think we'll get back into the Jensen home anytime soon," I pointed out.

"Mr. Jensen was supportive. They'll come around if Faith keeps causing problems."

I sat back in my chair, my dinner mostly uneaten. It was hard to have an appetite when a demon wanted you to sell your soul and ghosts were trying to relay a seemingly urgent message.

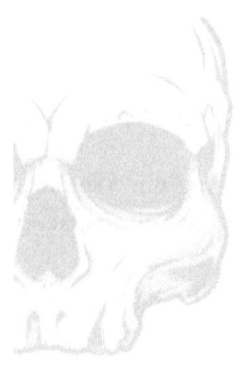

SEVENTEEN

I barely slept Tuesday night. My mind was so full of questions that I couldn't turn it off long enough to fall into a deep sleep. After Maxwell was banished, I thought that returning to my normal routine would help me recover from my grief. That hadn't even lasted for a week before life got complicated again.

Daisy and Shaun had made their feelings clear on what I should do about Tage and his offer. I wished I had someone else I could confide in, someone who was neutral enough to let me talk through the two possibilities before me.

But there was no one. Anyone close to me would instantly tell me to refuse Tage. Anyone not close to me would think I was absolutely crazy to be talking about demons and contracts with the Devil.

Maybe I was crazy.

No, I told myself, that's the kind of thing Tage wants me to think. Demons love chaos and making people question themselves and their understanding. I wouldn't fall prey to Tage's quiet manipulation.

Maybe there *was* someone who would listen to me, I realized. The one person I knew who didn't like me enough to really be concerned for my soul, but who understood that demons were a very real thing.

I called Carter.

He was as surprised about me calling him as I was, but I couldn't think of anyone else. I didn't explain much on the phone, saying only that I needed to talk over some paranormal things and that I needed a sounding board. Carter suggested we meet at a coffee shop, but I didn't want anyone overhearing us. Instead, I told him to come over to my apartment and I'd make the coffee myself.

Carter promised to come over the next night, which gave me twenty-four hours to second-guess my decision. I wasn't sure I had been right to even talk to Shaun and Daisy about the subject, let alone Carter. I guess I was worried that, if I agreed to sign the contract, everyone would somehow know. I'd be the girl that people pointed and laughed at, saying, "She's the one who sold her soul."

But, I thought, I'd have Maxwell by my side to stick up for me. At least, I assumed I would. What if I signed the contract and he came back, only to break up with me? No part of Tage's deal included a guarantee that Maxwell and I would live happily ever after.

These were the thoughts that I looked forward to articulating when Carter came over Wednesday night. First, though, I had to deal with his arrogance. He arrived at eight, and when I motioned him inside, his first words were, "It's tiny."

"It's historic," I countered.

"It's an old carriage house."

"It's an historic carriage house." He'd been inside for ten seconds, and already he was on my nerves. No wonder I'd had reservations about inviting Carter to my home. He probably lived in a palatial townhouse somewhere, and it was inevitable that he would find fault with my apartment.

I turned my back on Carter and walked into the kitchen. "Make yourself at home, if my couch isn't too tiny for you. You want coffee?"

"Please. Lots of sugar."

I took the few moments of quiet while I poured our coffee to breathe deeply. Carter didn't have much of a filter between his brain and his mouth. Neither did I, and of the two of us, I probably had the shorter fuse. I could let my mood escalate this into a disastrous evening, or I could calm down and be reasonable.

Calm and reasonable. I repeated those words as I handed Carter his mug. He looked unsure of himself, as if he didn't quite know how he came to be sitting on my couch. He was in dark gray slacks and a deep blue button-down shirt, and I had to admit that he was good-looking when his attitude didn't get in the way.

"Sorry if I snapped. It's been a really bad couple of weeks," I said.

"Yes, I assumed you wanted to meet me about the Jensen investigation."

"Actually, no. How do you know about that?"

"Carla Jensen called me to ask our team to investigate. Apparently your team went in and it got a little crazy. Carla seems to think it was your team's fault, but I don't think so."

"Are they still having problems?"

"They've repainted the little boy's room twice since The Seekers were there. Both times, words have shown up everywhere. They finally banned all paint, pens, pencils, and markers from the house, but the ghost used tomato juice instead."

"That poor family." It annoyed me that Carla still blamed Faith's behavior on us, like we had provoked the ghost somehow. Still, I felt sorry for the family as a whole, to be living with such a nuisance. "Have the words that Faith is writing changed?"

"It's the same ones, plus 'sweet dreams.'" Carter sipped

tentatively at his coffee. "Carla thinks the ghost is trying to talk to you."

I agreed, and I told Carter about the additional message coming through from the ghost children at the antique store. When I was done, he just shook his head. "You do seem to find trouble."

"It gets worse. None of this is why I even asked you to come over." I put down my coffee and folded my hands in my lap. I had turned sideways on the couch to face Carter, but I kept my eyes down as I spoke. "Maxwell was banished back to hell by a demon hunter."

"Oh." Carter was at a loss for words, a rare state for him. "I'm...so sorry."

"Apparently there's a way to bring Maxwell back."

Carter actually snickered. "What, do you have to sell your soul or something?"

"That's exactly what I have to do."

Carter's face instantly sobered, and he leaned forward. "Betty, you can't actually be considering it? He's a demon. I know you cared about him, but he's supposed to be in hell, not you."

"Please just hear me out. I keep running through both options in my head, and I just need to get it out. I can't make a decision until I've seriously weighed both choices."

Carter set his cup down and put his hands out, palms up. "Getting over the fact that your boyfriend is gone, and moving on with your life," he said, bouncing his left hand, "versus willingly sending your soul to hell for an eternity." Carter's right hand dropped, and I was surprised when he reached forward to take my hand. "You shouldn't be having a hard time weighing those options."

I shut my eyes. "I know. But please, Carter, hear me out. Let me talk this through."

Carter dropped my hand and settled back into the couch. "I'm listening."

I talked about every line of thought I'd had since Tage had come to see me on Sunday. I discussed my struggle between saving another's life and unleashing a demon on the world. I told Carter that if I said no, I worried that I would regret it for the rest of my life. What if every happy moment was tempered by thoughts of Maxwell and the suffering I'd been unwilling to prevent? Carter made it sound so easy, but getting over a banished boyfriend wasn't like moving on after a break-up.

Carter listened to me talk for nearly an hour. He barely spoke the whole time, stopping me only to ask a few questions. Whatever he was thinking, he didn't laugh or make fun of any of my fears. The only expression on his face was one of concern.

Finally, I was done. "So that's it," I told him. "That's why making a decision is harder than it seems."

"What if you and Maxwell had never started dating?" Carter asked. "Assume you didn't have a personal relationship with him, but that he was a demon wreaking havoc in a client's life. Would you call a demon hunter to come in and banish him?"

"I'd do it in a heartbeat," I admitted. "Maxwell is different, though. He's not all evil and destruction."

"Also, if Maxwell is a demon, he should be perfectly comfortable in hell. He's not a soul that's been sent there. It's like going back to his hometown. Why would an agent of Satan be suffering at all in hell?"

"Because he's being punished." The words hadn't come from me, but from somewhere over my right shoulder.

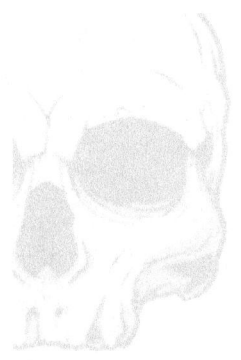

EIGHTEEN

I knew it was Tage without looking. Couldn't this guy learn to knock on a door? I whipped around and saw him walking from the kitchen.

"Another one?" Carter asked. He sounded more annoyed than afraid.

"I'll explain later," I said under my breath.

"Betty, how quickly you move on," Tage said, appraising Carter. "I must say, you do like men with money and good fashion sense."

Tage, on the other hand, was dressed in jeans and a Ramones tee-shirt. I considered explaining to him that Carter was far from a romantic interest, but there were more pressing matters at hand.

"Could you please use the front door next time?"

Okay, there were even more pressing matters than that, but I didn't want this guy just popping up in my apartment whenever he felt like it.

"I'll take that as an invitation to come back some other time. I'll leave you to your present company. Don't forget, Betty, I still need an answer from you."

We heard the pop this time as Tage dematerialized.

"I really can't stand that guy," I said.

Carter's response was to the point. "Explain."

So I did. I told him all about Maxwell's banishment

and how Tage helped guide me through the aftermath. I also explained that Tage was the one facilitating the sale of my soul.

"Can you negotiate?" Carter suddenly asked.

I stared blankly. "What?"

"The contract. Maybe you can bargain for only spending a little bit of time in hell, instead of eternity. Chances are, Maxwell's punishment won't last forever, and neither should yours."

"I hadn't thought of that." I considered for a moment, then smiled at Carter. "See? This is why I wanted to talk to you. Shaun and Daisy just said no, absolutely not, but you're giving me a new option. Thanks, Carter."

Carter actually looked a little flustered.

"Speaking of thanks," I continued, "it was really nice of you to hook Daisy up with that job."

"I just put her in touch with Dad's firm. She got the job on her own."

"How come you're being so nice to her?" I felt bad the moment I said it, but the words had come out before I could stop myself. Instead of accepting Carter's kindness toward my best friend, I had to question it.

"I wasn't aware that I'd ever been unkind. She's the one who pushed me down the stairs."

"Sorry. I didn't mean it to come out like that."

Carter shrugged. "It's just that the rivalry thing has gotten a little old. You're a better investigator than I'd expected, and we actually work pretty well together. There's still a lot you need to learn, but you've been good about following my lead."

I groaned. "Don't ruin this moment, Carter. You were doing so well there for a minute."

"I'm paying you a compliment."

"I'll take your word for it." I glanced at the clock and saw that it was already ten. I'd done so much talking that my throat felt dry and scratchy. "Thanks again for coming over tonight."

Carter realized that was his cue to leave, and I walked him to the door. "When are you going to investigate the Jensens' house?"

"Friday night. Do you want to come?"

"No way. Carla Jensen would have a fit if I went waltzing in there with your team. But please call me if anything happens. Tell the ghost you're a friend of mine, and maybe she'll tell you her message."

Carter opened my front door, but he turned back to me, his face serious. "Betty, please be careful. Between this ghost and the whole demon thing, you might really be in danger. I'll call you after the investigation to let you know what we learn."

"Thanks, Carter."

I don't know what had surprised me more that night: that Tage had materialized unannounced in my kitchen or that Carter had acted like a real, compassionate human being.

———◦✦◦———

My cell phone rang on Thursday while I was at work. Ordinarily that wouldn't be a big deal, except whomever was trying to reach me called ten times between one and three o'clock. I didn't recognize the number that popped up on the caller ID, so I ignored it each time. After all, I was working, and I didn't want to get in trouble for chatting on my cell while I was at the office. There was no voicemail following any of the calls, so I figured it was just some automated system calling to sell me something.

After attempt number ten, my phone was silent for the rest of the afternoon. The mysterious caller was long gone from my mind when my phone rang again during my drive home. It was the same number, and this time, I didn't have work as an excuse not to answer.

The voice on the other end belonged to Robyn, the girl from Holy Terrors Haunted House, but she sounded oddly tentative. She had been bold enough on the occasions we'd met her, until she'd gotten too up close and personal with a ghost, at least.

"I got your number from Azrael. I hope you don't mind," Robyn began. I assured her that she was welcome to call me (though not ten times in a row, I added silently), and she continued. "Remember I told you that I can sense things that others can't? Something really weird has started to happen to me, and I think it has something to do with you. I know that sounds strange."

I sighed. "Not as strange as you might think, Robyn. What's going on?"

"It's a long story. Can you come by Holy Terrors tonight?"

I promised I would be there by six so Robyn could talk to me before the haunted house opened at seven. That gave me just enough time to run home, slip into jeans and a long-sleeved shirt, put food in Mina's bowl, and head out again.

Robyn was altered when I saw her in the lobby of Holy Terrors. She looked as hesitant as she had sounded on the phone, and even her bright blue hair seemed subdued. "Thanks for coming," she said awkwardly. "Come on, we'll go sit somewhere quiet."

Robyn turned and walked into a hidden door that opened on a tunnel. She wended her way through several passages before pulling back a heavy black drape. I saw the cemetery scene beyond, still brightly lit, and she motioned for me to enter.

"This is definitely 'somewhere quiet,'" I said, trying to find some humor despite Robyn's drawn expression.

Robyn sat down on the floor, leaning up against a headstone. I joined her, folding my legs underneath me but staying away from the scenery: I was afraid I'd accidentally send one of the foam headstones toppling over. I didn't want to break the haunted house.

"So, what's been happening to you?" I prompted.

"It started as dreams," Robyn began. "I kept dreaming that a little girl was shouting at me, saying your name over and over again. It started around Monday night, and I'd wake up after I had the dream. Then, when I fell asleep again, I'd have the same dream."

"Are you still having the dream?"

"No. That only lasted through Tuesday night. Finally, I sat up in bed and yelled back, even though the girl was just a dream."

I couldn't help smiling at the thought. "What did you tell her?"

"That I got the damn message, and she could stop shouting at me." Robyn shrugged. "It worked; I stopped having the dream."

"But I assume something else happened."

"Yes. Az took all of us out Wednesday night. We were celebrating because we pulled in a record number of people last weekend. We went to Hannah's, that bar downtown. It's haunted, you know. I've gotten feelings in there before, and once felt someone whispering in my ear."

I nodded. I'd heard plenty of stories about the bar.

"I walked in the door, and it was like I'd been hit by a train." Robyn pushed her hands against her temples. "There was this wave of emotion that just ran over me. I suddenly felt claustrophobic, and really, really desperate. I've never felt anything like it before."

Robyn paused, lost in the memory, before she continued. "Then I heard a man talking to me, but it wasn't anyone there at Hannah's. It was a spirit; the one who haunts the place."

"What did he say?" I had to ask, even though I thought I knew what was coming.

"He said, 'Tell Betty,'" over and over. I got really frustrated and said, 'Tell her what?' It was pretty embarrassing because everyone turned and stared at me. He answered me, though, I guess. He said, 'Alive. Hope. Help.' That was it. After that, it was like he went away, and I felt normal again."

"'Alive. Hope. Help.'" I repeated. The "alive" was no surprise, but "hope" and "help" were new. I'd thought that Faith wanted to specify which Betty she meant, using "alive" to signify that it was me and not a ghost. The other words were an enigma. Did they mean there was hope for me if I got help? Or was I supposed to help someone else?

I was silent for a couple of minutes as I absorbed this new information. Robyn sat patiently, wrapping her arms around her knees and peering at me like I was an oddity. Finally, she broke the silence. "By the way, who is Maxwell?"

My head snapped up at that name, just as the overhead lights went out, plunging us into the absolute darkness of the cemetery scene.

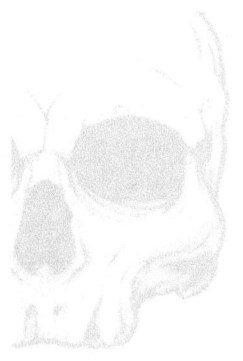

NINETEEN

I gasped, but Robyn let out a low, flat laugh. "Dramatic timing," she said. "It must be six-thirty. We always turn off the lights half an hour before we open our doors."

"How do you know about Maxwell?" I was leaning toward Robyn now, even though seeing anything in that darkness was futile. Her news of the dreams and the ghost at Hannah's had been mysterious, but it hadn't made my heart race the way her casual mention of Maxwell had.

"I had another dream last night. That same little girl came back to shout at me some more. She's a precocious little thing, isn't she? She must be a ghost. I wonder if she was like that when she was alive. You know, really persistent and used to getting attention when she wanted it."

I was going to be doing some shouting of my own if Robyn didn't tell me about Maxwell.

"Anyway, this time, instead of saying your name, she said, 'Maxwell.' Again, and again, and again, like I was too stupid to get it the first time. When I woke up, I told her thanks, and that I'd gotten the message. The dream didn't come back."

I was silent.

"So who is Maxwell, anyway? Was he that guy you came through here with? It was dark, but he looked pretty hot."

"He was my boyfriend, but not anymore."

"Oh, I'm sorry. Breaking up sucks."

"Yeah."

"We'd better get going. I've got to slap on my zombie makeup so I can get in position before we open." Robyn shuffled to her feet before a dim light emanated from her hand. She had a tiny flashlight with a red bulb in it, and she pointed the way toward the curtained doorway through which we'd entered. She moved with ease, clearly more comfortable and familiar with the darkness than I was.

Robyn escorted me to the lobby, where a few early arrivals were already waiting to buy their tickets. The lights showed that Robyn had recovered some of her spunk, as if unburdening herself had helped her regain some of her usual confidence. I, on the other hand, probably looked weary and thoughtful. It was how I felt, at least.

"What do you think it all means?" Robyn said.

"I wish I knew. I think the little girl you dreamed of was Faith, a ghost who haunts a Victorian home. It seems like she's trying to get a message to me, but we can't figure out what it is. It's like she's having a hard time communicating."

"I'll call if I have any more dreams."

"Please do. And thank you, Robyn. I appreciate you telling me all of this."

Robyn nodded, then reached forward and drew me into a hug. "Something is wrong," she whispered into my ear. "I could feel that much from the little girl and from the ghost at Hannah's. You need to be careful."

Intuitive people can be so annoyingly mysterious sometimes.

Still, I knew Robyn was trying to be helpful, even though her tale had given me more questions instead of some answers. I sat in my car for a long time, going over her story and the other messages from Faith. I couldn't make any sense of the jumble of words, so I pulled a notebook out of my purse and wrote them all down.

"Betty" was, of course, me. And there was no doubt that it was my Maxwell who was a part of the message. After all, he had lived in the same house as Faith, though his residence there was after her death in the home. "Alive. Hope. Help." I wrote the words, each on their own line with a big question mark after them.

"Sweet dreams" was at the bottom of the list. I ran my finger lightly over the words, remembering the way Maxwell's voice had always been so low, so smooth, when he said those words to me. He never told me, "Good night." It was always, "Sweet dreams."

The words suddenly clicked into place and I uttered a startled "Oh!"

Maxwell was alive.

I sat for a few minutes, my heart desperately trying to leap out of my chest. I felt elated yet uncertain. It couldn't be that simple. I had seen Maxwell banished to hell, and Tage had confirmed it. The demon hunter had even apologized, in his own self-righteous way, for breaking my heart.

But the words certainly indicated that Maxwell was still alive and trying to get a message to me via Faith and her paranormal network. No one but Maxwell and I knew he said "sweet dreams" to me. And the repeated "alive" had seemed so redundant in reference to me, but it made sense that Faith was trying to hammer home the fact that someone I'd thought was lost actually wasn't.

"Hope" and "help" suddenly took on new meaning. If Maxwell was alive, then there was hope for him, and it seemed he was reaching out to me for help. But help how? If he was alive, then why wasn't he here with me? He could be in hiding, fearing that the demon hunter would return. Or, I reasoned, he could be hiding to keep the demon hunter from coming after me.

The theory that Maxwell was alive certainly left me with plenty of questions. The biggest of them was, of course, how could I not have realized it sooner? It seemed obvious now, but I'd been convinced that Maxwell was really and truly banished. I had no reason to even consider that he might, in fact, be involved with this haunting.

How could Tage, the demon hunter, and I all have been wrong about Maxwell's banishment? Unless, of course, his banishment had been only temporary. Maybe he'd escaped hell or bargained his way out. That still didn't explain why he'd need my help.

I sat in my car so long, going over the questions again and again, that the teenagers who had parked next to me had already gone through Holy Terrors and left before I stirred.

I drove straight to Shaun and Daisy's house. I didn't even call to warn them I was coming.

Shaun looked at me quizzically when he answered the door. "Betty? You okay?"

"No."

"Tell us." Shaun opened the door wide and ushered me into the living room. I had no sooner sunk down on the couch than Daisy swooped over me, her hands fluttering over my head and shoulders as if she might find a physical injury.

"Nothing bad has happened," I said, swatting at Daisy's hands. "I'm fine in that sense. It's Faith. She's gotten more talkative."

In her usual style of Southern hospitality, Daisy wouldn't let me speak until I had a glass of sweet tea in my hand. Her formality ended there. "Out with it, Boo!" she said.

I related Robyn's tale, as well as my revelation. Daisy

listened with stunned silence, but Shaun kept interrupting with questions like, "Are you sure that's what it means?" and "Can we really trust this ghost at Hannah's? We don't even know him."

Despite Shaun's interjections, I managed to get through my whole story before I'd gotten halfway through my iced tea. Daisy was keenly aware of my slow sipping, and her first comment when I'd finished talking was, "Did it not have enough sugar?"

"What?"

"The tea. You've hardly had any."

"Daze, it's fine. I'm just distracted."

Daisy let out her breath in a huff. "You must be really upset, then, if you're not in the mood for my sweet tea."

I pointedly took a giant gulp of the drink, raising my eyebrows to say, "See? I'm fine."

But I was far from fine, and Daisy and Shaun both knew it. I put my glass down and sighed. "I feel like I'm being strung along," I said. "First Maxwell was banished and gone forever, then he was banished but could come back, and now he's alive. Well, which is it? Somebody must know the truth."

"At least each report gives you more hope," Shaun said gently.

"It was almost easier when I had no hope. All this speculation and possibility is killing me. I hope it's true, but what if it's not? I don't want to deal with the grief of losing Maxwell again because I have a false hope in something a ghost said."

"Might have said. You're assuming your interpretation of the words is correct." Daisy's voice was sympathetic.

"It's the only explanation I can come up with. 'Sweet dreams' is what Maxwell always said to me. How would anyone know that?"

"You do have a ghost in your apartment, and you said

that they can communicate with one another. Maybe Faith heard the phrase from your Spirit Sentry," Shaun said.

I shrugged. He had a point, which I acknowledged before adding, "It still means that Faith's message has something to do with Maxwell."

Daisy moved closer to me and put her arm around my shoulders. "Do you think the other demon could have something to do with it? Maybe he's trying to drive you crazy."

I thought for a long moment. To Daisy's delight, I drained my glass as I did so. She had already gotten the pitcher of tea from the kitchen, refilled my glass, returned the pitcher to the refrigerator, and resumed her seat before I spoke. "I don't think Tage is involved in this. He wants me to sell my soul. Whatever the truth may be, Tage wants me to believe that Maxwell is in hell, and that I'm the only one who can do anything about it."

"If that's the case," Shaun said, "then Tage is either lying to you, or he doesn't know the truth, either. I wonder which it is."

"Next time he pops up, I'll ask him," I promised.

As it turned out, I didn't have to wait very long at all.

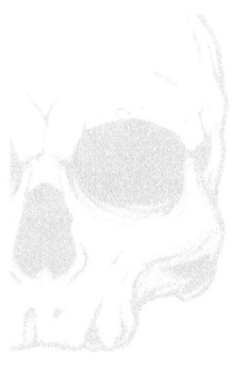

TWENTY

I was sitting at my desk on Friday afternoon, tapping my toe impatiently. I couldn't concentrate at all because my thoughts were focused on Maxwell and I'd barely slept the night before. The result was that I had gotten nearly nothing accomplished all day, but one glance in the mirror proved that I had the appearance of working myself to exhaustion.

It's a good thing Maxwell isn't around to see me, I thought dryly. He'd be horrified. I rubbed my eyes and stifled a yawn. The cursor on my computer screen hadn't moved for twenty minutes.

The phone on my desk rang three times before I picked it up. I was feeling so languid that I nearly let it go to voice-mail. The receptionist's voice was on the other end of the line, her perkiness in sharp contrast to my weariness.

"Betty, there's a man here to see you," Jeanie said. Her voice lowered to a hiss and she added, "He's very mysterious."

I instantly thought of Maxwell, and before I could think, I said, "Oh, send him back!" There was no way it could be Maxwell, but it was too late to take back my outburst: Jeanie had already hung up.

I patted my hair and quickly checked my makeup in a compact I kept in my desk. I was going to look bad no matter what, but I'd at least do what I could to look less bad. No one ever visited me at work, so I felt like I was preparing for a special occasion. I just wished that I knew who would be walking through my door.

It took me a moment to recognize Tage when he sauntered into my office. He was wearing a gray suit, and his hair was styled with more care than he'd shown on previous visits.

I must have looked surprised because Tage said, "I know, I do clean up well, don't I?" He turned and shut my office door in one fluid motion before settling into the sole visitor's chair that I had. Only fellow employees had ever occupied it.

"This is unexpected," I finally managed.

"You asked that I cease my impromptu visits to your apartment. I thought a more formal meeting might put you at ease."

"Not really." My office suddenly felt much too small. It had always been cramped, but now the walls seemed to be closing in, and I wondered if this is what it felt like to be thrown into a cage with a hungry lion.

"Betty, let me cut straight to the chase. I need to know if you are going to sell your soul in exchange for Maxwell's salvation."

"I can't answer that," I said firmly.

"I grow very tired of waiting. Delay much longer, and my offer will expire."

"I can't give you my answer until you've told me the truth."

Tage sat up just a little straighter. My frankness was clearly a surprise to him. "Do tell," he said smoothly.

"Where is Maxwell?"

"In hell, of course. The fiery pit."

"No; he's alive."

Tage actually laughed. "Oh, Betty, don't fool yourself.

Has your hope revived even after witnessing his banishment yourself? You are more affected than I thought if you believe such nonsense."

"Someone told me that Maxwell is still alive," I insisted. I wasn't going to let Tage's careless dismissal of the matter get to me. I had to stick to my point.

"Then *someone* must want you to suffer needlessly."

"You said that when Maxwell was banished, you just knew. You could feel it because you're both demons and because he was your friend. If that's true, then surely you can feel where he is now. He must be hiding somewhere."

Tage leaned forward and rested his forearms on my desk. He gaze was intense as he said, "If, hypothetically, he were alive, why would he be in hiding?"

"I don't know. Maybe he's afraid the demon hunter who tried to kill him is still around and might discover him. He could be injured and unable to materialize back home. Please, Tage, I need to find him."

"There is only one place to find him, but you won't ever see that place until your soul has parted from your flesh. Betty, you are confused and upset. Don't cling to false hope. It will only prolong your suffering."

I nodded and broke my eyes away from Tage's. His stare was almost hypnotic, like Maxwell's, only much more sinister. Tage was going to stick to his claim that Maxwell was in hell. As Shaun had said, he was either lying to me, or he really thought Maxwell had been banished. It would be impossible for me to determine which was true. Clearly, though, I would get no help from Tage in finding Maxwell. It was Tage's word against Faith's, I realized, and I would trust a ghost over a demon any day.

If he were truly Maxwell's friend, I thought, Tage would want to help me search for him. Then again, maybe the prospect of claiming a soul for hell meant more than friendship to Tage.

"I need your answer," Tage finally said. His voice was quiet, coaxing.

"I can't give it to you yet," I said, bringing my eyes back to his. "Not now."

Tage's calm was replaced by anger. He stood, his eyes glinting. "That will not do. You must answer me."

I thought quickly. Carter and his team were going to investigate the Jensen home tonight. If they could get more answers, then maybe I could give my own answer to Tage. "I need another two days," I said.

"Fine. On Sunday, you decide," he said firmly. "If you still cannot make up your mind, then our deal is off. Your lover will burn in hell for eternity, and it will be your fault."

Tage heaved a deep breath and smoothed his jacket.

"What happens to me if I say no?" I asked.

Tage glared down at me. "Don't say no."

Our conversation was clearly at an end. I expected him to walk out of my office, but instead he leveled one final, menacing look at me and dematerialized.

He had been gone only a split second before I was up out of my chair and opening my office door. The air of the hallway felt cool and refreshing compared to the suffocating atmosphere of my office. I walked briskly down the hall, feeling the need to distance myself from my office as much as possible. When I got to the front desk, Jeanie nearly pounced on me in her eagerness.

"So who was the handsome guy?" she asked, putting a caller on hold so she could catch my attention.

"It's a long story, and he's not at all handsome," I said, indicating with a wave that she should return to her phone duties.

Jeanie transferred the call in record time and called out to me again before I could escape her presence. "Where did he go? Is he still in your office?"

"No. He, uh, must have gone out the side door."

"You still haven't told me who he was."

"Oh, he was a friend of a friend who died recently," I lied. Well, it was mostly a lie.

Jeanie's face fell. "Oh, Betty, I'm so sorry. I didn't know. Are you okay?"

"I'm okay. He stopped by because he thought I was having a hard time dealing with it, but I'm all right."

Of course, I wasn't all right. I was still mystified about Maxwell's whereabouts and how I could help him. Or, for that matter, why he even needed help in the first place.

I was also very aware that I only had forty-eight hours before I had to decide the fate of my soul. If Carter and his team didn't get some more firm answers during their investigation, I honestly had no idea what I would tell Tage. I knew he wouldn't take a "no" very well, and while I might get out of a one-way trip to hell, I might also get a quick one-way trip to dead.

Never in my life had I wished Carter so much good fortune, and never had I been more apprehensive about his skills as a ghost hunter.

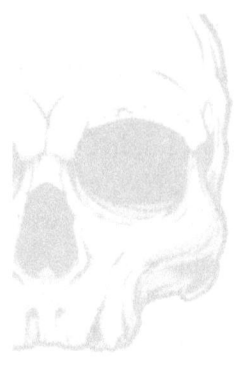

TWENTY-ONE

After some inner debate, I called and asked Carter to stop by my apartment before he went on the Jensen investigation that night. On one hand, I didn't want to alarm Carter with the news that his investigation might determine my fate. On the other hand, I thought that the knowledge might make him that much more conscientious in his night's work. I was pacing back and forth in my living room when he knocked on my door.

"Twice in one week," Carter said in greeting.

"Faith has been busy, and you need to know what she's been up to," I answered, waving Carter toward my couch.

He sat down with a frown. "I would have expected the Jensens to call me with any news of their ghost."

"They probably don't know about this. Remember Robyn, the girl with blue hair who works at Holy Terrors? Faith appeared to her in a dream."

Carter's frown deepened, and I brought him up to date on everything that had occurred over the past two days. He was the first person I told about Tage's visit to my office and my promise of delivering an answer on Sunday. Normally I would have unburdened myself on Daisy, but since there was nothing she could do to help in the matter, I saw no point in making her worry needlessly.

When I finished, Carter leaned back and stared up at

my ceiling. He was quiet for a full minute before I got impatient and said, "Well?"

"Well…it's a lot of pressure on us," he said quietly.

"I thought maybe you could ask specific questions about Maxwell to see if we can find out where he is or what kind of help he needs."

"We can, and we will. You're assuming, though, that you've interpreted these words correctly. Ghosts can be very cryptic." Carter's voice took on a lecturer's tone, and I rolled my eyes at him.

"This is not a good time to tell me I'm wrong," I warned.

"I'm not saying you're wrong. I'm just warning you to be cautious. Don't jump to conclusions."

"I think it's too late for that. Maxwell is alive, I know it."

"In that case, you have no reason to sell your soul. You already have your answer for the demon, no matter what my team finds tonight."

"Well, I still want to make sure that my theory is right."

"You just said it was."

"But what if it's not? If I refuse to sell my soul, but I'm wrong about Maxwell, then he'll never get out of hell." And here I'd been so sure of myself.

"If you do sell your soul, only to find out Maxwell is still alive, then you'll have given up your soul for nothing," Carter added.

"Exactly. So you can see why I'm still having a hard time juggling these conjectures and monumental decisions." I leaned forward and cradled my head in my hands. I'd started getting a headache as soon as Tage had left my office, and it felt like every worry I had was trying to chisel its way out of my skull.

"We'll do our best tonight, I promise," Carter said.

"And if we get any scrap of evidence tonight, I'll call you right away and tell you."

"Thanks."

Carter was silent until I sat back up. "Did you ever ask the demon about getting eternity in hell downgraded to just a short visit?"

I shook my head. "No, but I have the feeling he's the type who doesn't compromise. And if I do tell him no, then I think he'll retaliate somehow."

"You do find danger, Betty."

"Yeah, it does like to pop right up in the middle of my living room."

I saw Carter out with more pleas that his team would try to find out details about Maxwell, and he gave me more assurances. I kept chattering nervously until Carter walked out the door. He paused and turned to point a stern finger at me. "Call Daisy, or Shaun, or anybody who can keep you company tonight. You shouldn't be alone."

Carter left without another word, and I was left to wonder if he really thought I was in danger. If so, was it from Tage or myself? Carter was right; I needed some company to keep me from getting too worked up.

I hadn't gotten past the thought of pulling out my cell phone when there was another knock on my door. It was Daisy, and I saw Shaun and Lou behind her. Shaun's head was bent toward Carter's, who hadn't made it five feet from my door. The two were talking in low voices, but Shaun's urgency and Carter's astonishment were apparent.

"What's going on?" I asked. "How did you know I was about to call?"

"Oh, did she call you, too?" Daisy asked.

"Who?"

"Carla Jensen."

"No. I was just going to call you to ask for some company tonight."

"You'll have company in spades. We're all going to the Jensen investigation."

I frowned and looked toward Carter, whose expression was now a mixture of annoyance and concern.

"But Carter's team is going tonight." Now I was feeling panicked *and* confused.

Daisy called Carter to come back inside, and as they all filed across my threshold, Lou caught my arm in a firm grip. He looked down at me gravely but said nothing.

Soon Daisy had the four of us seated around my little dining room table, and she stood before us like a schoolteacher. "Carla Jensen called me about an hour ago. Carter, I know you're probably mad, but hear me out. Carla's youngest son woke up this morning and said that Faith really needed to talk to Betty. He claimed that he talked to Faith during the night, but Carla dismissed it as a dream. When she came home from work, there was more writing all over the walls and furniture, but it was in every bedroom this time. She wants The Seekers there since Faith seems to want to talk to Betty directly."

"Why can't Betty just go with my team tonight then? Why do all of you have to go?" Carter was angry, though I could tell he was trying to suppress it.

Daisy's voice was firm. "Faith is drawing all over three bedrooms now. Carla thought you'd need all the extra manpower you can get."

"She should have called me since it's my investigation," Carter said, pursing his lips. I hid a smile: it was kind of nice to see Carter being himself again. How quickly he slid back into his arrogant mannerisms.

"You're right, she should have," Shaun agreed. "But I doubt Carla, or anyone in that family, is really thinking with a clear head right now."

Carter grumbled something under his breath and stood up. "Let's get it over with, then."

I quickly changed into a Seekers tee and grabbed my paranormal pack. Daisy and Shaun offered to give me a ride to the Jensens', but I winked at Daisy as I answered, "No, thanks. I thought I'd go with Carter so he could have some company."

I'm not sure if Carter appreciated the gesture or if it made him more angry. I had to admit I was getting a strange amount of satisfaction from Carter's attitude. Everything else in my life seemed crazy, so it was nice to have something as constant and familiar as Carter's snobbery.

His demeanor didn't last long, though. One look at Carla and Scott Jensen quickly sobered all of us. Carla looked slightly wild, her hair disheveled and her wide eyes ringed with streaked mascara. Scott was quiet, and his shoulders slumped in defeat. I was briefly filled with a strong desire to turn and run off their front step. I was anxious for news of Maxwell, but the Jensens' appearance gave me some doubts of getting anything useful at all. They looked tormented, not enlightened.

Carla stared accusingly at me as we silently sat down in the living room. I could feel my cheeks burning red with embarrassment, and I averted my eyes. What was I supposed to do? Apologize because a ghost wanted to tell me something?

Since it was Carter's investigation, I was happy—for once—to let him run things his way. The rest of his team included a couple named Ron and Kerry, and they had arrived before us. Carter had quickly issued instructions for them to begin hauling in their video cameras and monitors, but Carla had only laughed sardonically at this.

"It won't do you any good," she said.

"Why do you say that?" Carter asked.

"Because the damage has already been done. There's nothing left for you to capture on film."

I noticed that Scott had one arm around his wife's shoulders, but his torso was leaning away from her, as if he wanted to distance himself. "It won't hurt to set up the cameras, anyway," he said quietly. Carla snorted in answer, but Ron and Kerry were soon hauling heavy cases marked "East Coast Paranormal Authorities" into the house.

Lou jumped up to help, which left just Shaun, Daisy, Carter, and me to hear the report of the latest paranormal activity.

Carla summed it up, saying, "You just have to go upstairs and see it." She refused to say more, and Scott hedged around Carter's questions, as well. Apparently, it really did have to be seen to be believed.

There was no sense in asking more questions, so Carter allowed Carla and Scott to lead us upstairs. We went into Derek's bedroom first. The youngest Jensen son had already endured so many of Faith's demonstrations that he and his brother had been dispatched to their grandparents' again.

Derek's room was, as before, covered in writing. The walls—a crisp and freshly-painted white—were covered from floor to ceiling in Faith's familiar childish scrawl. The desk, the chair, the headboard: every piece repainted, and every piece again covered in writing.

I was hardly surprised to see the words covering all of the surfaces: "Tell Betty." The phrase screamed at me over and over, and I felt like shouting back that I was listening and ready to hear the message.

Carla and Scott then led us into Bryan's room. It was the same scene, except the letters spelled "Help Maxwell."

As I stared at the message repeated hundreds, if not thousands, of times all over the bedroom, I unconsciously brought my hand to my chest, as if my heart might leap out at any moment. Tears instantly sprang to my eyes, and

I wondered what agony Maxwell was in that gave Faith so much urgency.

Daisy gave me a pat on the back, and her sympathy finally broke my calm. I cried openly, at once conscious of everyone staring at me, yet not caring one bit. Daisy wrapped her arms around me, whispering, "We'll find him, Betty."

When my tears slowed to a more manageable trickle, I wiped at my eyes with the back of my hand and mumbled an apology to the others. Even Carla looked slightly less bitter toward me, and she asked, "Does the name mean something to you? You mentioned the name before, that he was an owner of this house once."

I nodded, but no words would come. Carter spoke up for me. "Maxwell was also the name of Betty's boyfriend, who's…gone missing. We're beginning to suspect that whatever Faith wants to communicate has to do with him."

"Oh. I'm terribly sorry," Carla said. She actually sounded like she meant it, and I figured I was finally making some headway with her.

When I recovered my voice, I said, "What's in the third bedroom?"

"Maybe you should go downstairs and wait," Scott said to me.

"No, I'm fine. Let's go."

The room we entered was the master bedroom, and I expected to see the antique four-poster bed and furnishings covered in the same repeated lines.

Instead, there was only one word, written across one wall in huge red letters: PRISONER.

I didn't cry this time. I threw up my arm to ward off the word, which seemed to leap at me from the pale lavender wall.

"What does it mean?" I heard Shaun say. His voice seemed very far away.

"It means Maxwell is a prisoner. That's why he needs help." Daisy was the one who supplied the answer, articulating what I could not. I soon felt her hand in mine. "You can open your eyes, Betty," she whispered.

I did, but I kept them pointed at the carpet. "A prisoner of whom?" My voice was so quiet that only Daisy heard me, and she repeated the question to the others.

No one had an answer, and I could only hope that Faith would give us some insight.

With that in mind, we trooped downstairs. The kitchen was our base of operations again, and it was a crowded spot with all of us in there. Ron and Kerry took infrared cameras upstairs to film the bedrooms, while Lou guided their work from his post at the monitor. "Left, a little more left, now up a bit," he said into his radio.

Shaun and Carter were discussing the meaning of the words written in the three rooms when Daisy interjected, "Could it be a demon hunter keeping Maxwell prisoner?" She kept her voice low enough so Carla and Scott wouldn't overhear—they insisted on staying with us for the entire investigation—but Lou caught her words. He spun around abruptly, his radio temporarily forgotten.

"No way," he said firmly. "They wouldn't do something like that. It's not protocol."

I raised my eyebrows. "Do you know a lot about their protocol?"

Lou started, but momentarily answered, "Enough to know that would never happen. It's too big of a risk. Besides, what would be the point?"

"To study his behavior," Daisy suggested.

"Torture," Carter said. He glanced at me, his face grim.

"I'm inclined to believe Lou," I said slowly. "When I saw the hunter at the cathedral, he was convinced of his success. I didn't get any sense that he was lying to me."

"He might be a man of God, but he's still capable of lying," Shaun warned.

I shook my head. "No, I can usually tell when someone's lying to me."

"That's true," Shaun agreed. "I tried to lie to you about that surprise birthday party we planned when you turned 21 and failed miserably."

I smiled briefly at the memory. "At least I still acted surprised when I arrived." I could see the looks of confusion on Carla and Scott's faces, so I cleared my throat and eyed Carter. He took the hint and began outlining our plan.

"Betty, you and I in the first bedroom. Derek's, I believe. Ron and Kerry will take the second one, and Shaun and Daisy will start in the master bedroom. That's a lot of us up there on the second floor, so everyone be as quiet as possible. Once you get in the room, don't move around a lot or talk loudly. We don't want to get false audio evidence because someone was stamping their feet."

I grabbed my camera and tape recorder, and Carter snagged a radio for us. I was glad he'd put us in Derek's room. "Tell Betty" was a lot more tolerable than "Help Maxwell" and "PRISONER."

We shut off the lights in the bedroom and settled down onto the floor in front of Derek's nightstand.

"What do you think she used for ink?" I mused. "I thought they took all the pens and markers out of the house."

"No idea."

The noise of everyone else getting situated died down until we had near silence. The only sounds were the occasional car on the street outside and the hum of the air conditioning.

At my request, Carter radioed downstairs and asked that the air be turned off. We didn't want its noise drowning out any EVPs, and I certainly didn't want to mistake the air current as some kind of paranormal breeze.

"The EVP session is all yours," Carter said.

Of course it was. If Faith really wanted to talk to me, then she ought to respond to my voice. But then, we'd tried that before and it hadn't really worked. Was Faith just being obstinate that night or was something keeping her from communicating clearly?

There was a longer break than usual between my questions. If Faith was having trouble communicating, I wanted to give her plenty of time to respond. Even though I knew I was unlikely to hear anything with my own ears, I strained to discern something in the silence. It only served to worsen my headache. Still, I continued to listen, knowing my only chance of hearing something would be on the tape recorder.

So I was really surprised when a soft, high voice demanded, "Don't!" right into my ear.

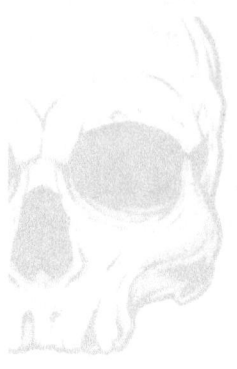

TWENTY-TWO

"Don't what?" I asked. I sat up straight, looking around me for the source of the voice.

"Pardon?" Carter asked.

I grabbed his arm and squeezed, and he understood that I didn't want him to make a sound. "Don't what?" I asked again, louder this time.

There was no response. I tried framing the question in other ways, but each time the silence stretched until I gave up on hearing that insistent little voice again. I realized I was still clenching Carter's arm, and I slowly uncurled my fingers. "I think Faith spoke to me," I explained. "A voice said, 'Don't,' right into my ear."

Carter was immediately on the radio down to Lou. "Make a note to recheck the video feed from bedroom one over the past five minutes or so. Betty heard a voice."

Sadly, that was the only occurrence during the course of the long night. We were there until three o'clock, but it was a quiet, disappointing vigil. And, once again, I had another question to answer. What had Faith meant? It would be a whole lot easier if this ghost could actually communicate in whole sentences.

By the time Carter dropped me off at my apartment, I was exhausted, both physically and mentally. My head was still pounding, so I swallowed some aspirin and flopped into bed.

I was so tired that I slept soundly all night long and, for the first time since it had happened, I didn't dream of Maxwell's banishment.

Saturday was a big blank on my calendar: there were no investigations, no plans, and nowhere to go. It was glorious. I lingered over my morning coffee, sipping it in the courtyard between my carriage house apartment and the historic home to which it belonged. I had to put on a cardigan to do so since the chill of fall was in the morning air, but I didn't care. The sun was shining, I could listen to the clatter of horses' hooves as carriages full of tourists passed by on the street, and I had a book to distract me from my cares for a while.

All too soon, though, I lost interest in my book and began thinking about Maxwell again. It startled me when I realized that I was actually more concerned about his whereabouts and well being than I was about the future of my own soul. But if I could find Maxwell and know he really was alive, then I would know what to tell Tage.

Tage. Just thinking about the demon gave me a shiver. I had only twenty-four hours before he would expect an answer from me. What was I going to tell him? And what would he do if he didn't like my answer?

I had hoped for some better answers from Faith, but that one word, "PRISONER," supported my belief that Maxwell had not, in fact, been banished. Someone was keeping him a prisoner. For what reason, I didn't know.

As Saturday afternoon wore on, I tried to distract myself with an old musical that was being shown on TV, but even that didn't help.

I jumped when my cell phone rang, and I had to laugh at myself for being a little too on edge. It was Lou, and he had some interesting—if puzzling—evidence to share. He had taken my tape recorder, as well as Shaun and Daisy's, to analyze our EVP sessions. Ron and Kerry had gone home with all of theirs, plus Carter's.

"I don't know what it means, Boo," Lou said, "but at least we did get an EVP. Listen." There was a shuffling sound as Lou moved his phone next to his computer speakers. Soon I heard a high voice, the same I'd heard in my ear, say, "Thirty, one-fifth, thirty, one-fifth, thirty, one-fifth…" It went on for at least twenty seconds, going right over a question I had asked. Faith spoke so quickly that the words all ran together.

"Well?" Lou asked, putting the phone back up to his ear.

"What is that supposed to mean?"

"You've got me."

"I really wish Faith could be less mysterious. Hey, by any chance, did you get her voice saying, 'Don't'?"

Lou sighed. "No. We don't have any evidence of that. But if she was speaking up close to your ear, then the tape recorder might have been too far away to pick it up."

"Thanks, Lou."

"Betty," Lou said, and paused.

"Yes?"

"God bless you." Lou hung up before I could respond.

So now I had yet another mysterious message to interpret and no idea where to begin. Thirty and one-fifth what? Was it an increment of time? A measurement? The number of glasses of wine I'd need before I felt less miserable?

I had so much on my mind that I was halfway through making dinner when I realized it had been exactly two weeks since Maxwell's banishment. Or, rather, disappearance, since he apparently hadn't been banished at all. It had been a busy two weeks.

Carter called me at nine o'clock, so frantic that I could hardly understand him.

"Carter, you have to slow down. I have to what?"

Carter took a deep breath. "You need to come over to Ron and Kerry's to hear the EVPs they got."

"Can't you tell me over the phone?"

"I could, but I want you to hear them yourself. One of them is a strange word we can't really make out, and we need an unbiased opinion."

Carter gave me directions and I promised to be there within twenty minutes. Kerry and Ron shared an apartment on the Southside, and during my drive I called Daisy to fill her in. Lou had played the puzzling EVP for her, too, and she was also stumped as to its meaning. I promised to call her back after I checked out what the East Coast Paranormal Authorities had captured.

The apartment complex was easy enough to find, but every building looked alike and I'm pretty sure the builders purposely posted the unit numbers behind trees. My patience was wearing thin by the time I found the right building.

Kerry answered the door with her usual bland demeanor. She was a little standoffish toward me, but it was a lot less obvious than Carter's flagrant snobbery. Ron and Carter, at least, greeted me with a little more enthusiasm.

I skipped right past a greeting and said, "So what have you found?"

"Here's the first," Ron said. He was already seated at a computer desk tucked in a corner of the little dining room, and he had the first audio clip already cued for me.

Carter, who had gone to the master bedroom with Shaun later in the night, was the first to speak on the recording. "What is it you're trying to tell Betty?" he asked.

The reply was faint, and I heard an inaudible whisper.

"This is the one we can't make out," Ron explained. "Here, try listening with a headset."

I put the proffered headset on and closed my eyes in concentration. This time, the whisper took on a form that made me cry out in surprise. "Play it again!" I said.

Ron played it through twice more, and there was no doubt about the word. Faith said it quietly, timidly almost.

"Tage."

I pulled off the headphones and repeated the word with as much temerity. How was the demon related to our investigation?

"Is that a name?" Kerry asked, too bored to even look up from the fingernail she was filing.

My eyes flicked to Carter. His mouth hung open, and he would have looked comical in a less unsettling situation. "Why him?" Carter asked.

I could only shrug. "Play the next one, please."

Ron obliged, pulling up the next clip for me. I heard Kerry's voice ask, "Where are you?" It seemed like an odd question to me, but apparently it was the right one to ask. Faith's response came quickly and clearly: "Atlanta."

I expected Faith to repeat the word, but she said it only once, clearly and succinctly.

"Faith is in Atlanta?" I asked.

Carter responded slowly, as if I were a child trying to understand a complex idea. "We think it might be where Maxwell is."

"How are we supposed to find him in a city of that size?" I said. "And why would he be in Atlanta?" A sudden thought struck me, and I snatched my purse from the edge of the computer table. "I have to go home and check something. I'll call you soon."

"No way," Carter said. "I'm going with you."

I was in too much of a hurry to argue. I probably broke several traffic laws on my way home, and more than once I heard a gasp from Carter as I made questionable passes. There was no slowing me down once I parked, either. I dashed into my apartment and headed straight for my laundry hamper. There at the bottom, hidden by all my dirty clothes, were the few keepsakes of Maxwell's that I'd kept.

I pulled out his cell phone and turned it on, hoping it still had a charge. All I needed was enough battery to check one fact.

I let out my breath when it powered up and clumsily found my way to Maxwell's address book. I found the entry for Tage and saw his 770 area code.

"Tage lives in Atlanta," I said.

"So that means…" Carter was leaning against the doorframe, frowning at the dirty clothes I'd scattered everywhere.

"It means that Tage is the one holding Maxwell prisoner."

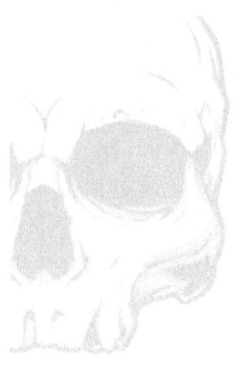

TWENTY-THREE

Somehow I wound up sitting on my couch. I could hear Carter saying, "You need to get here right away. No, she'll be okay." I was in such shock over the realization that Maxwell was in Tage's custody that I had just blanked out for a minute.

The next thing I knew, Carter was pressing a glass of water into my hand. I looked up and saw the worry on his face, and I patted his arm. "Don't worry, I'm not going to pass out on you."

"It was pretty creepy how your eyes glassed over after you looked at the demon's phone number."

"Where is the phone?"

"You dropped it somewhere. Hang on." Carter retrieved the cell phone while I got up and fished my notebook out of my paranormal pack. I wanted to get Tage's phone number written down before Maxwell's phone went dead. After all, Tage and I had a few things to discuss.

I didn't know where to begin. Now we knew that Maxwell was being held prisoner by Tage and that they were somewhere in Atlanta. I wasn't sure what we could do short of going door to door through a city of millions and asking, "Have you seen this demon?"

To clear my head, I turned to the page of my notebook that held all of Faith's communications so far. I had already added the words we saw during Friday night's investigation. Underneath those, I wrote "thirty, one-fifth, Atlanta."

Daisy arrived before long, but she'd brought the cavalry with her. Shaun and Lou both trailed after her, and I was soon surrounded by three worried faces.

"I'm okay, I'm okay," I said, waving everyone back. "I had a little moment there when I felt kind of out of it."

Daisy looked down at the notebook in my lap. "Oh! It's an address."

She explained when I just stared blankly in response. "It's not 'thirty' and 'one-fifth.' It's '31 Fifth.' It's an address in Atlanta."

My eyes widened. "You think?"

"Let's check," Lou said. He found my laptop on the dining room table and pulled up a map of Atlanta. He repeated the address quietly to himself as he typed it into the search window.

After a few moments, Lou let out a satisfied, "Hah!" and spun the laptop around so we could see the screen. "It's right there," he said, pointing at a spot.

"We know where Maxwell is," I said. I couldn't believe it. As much as I'd hoped Faith would point us to him, I hadn't expected her to give us such a detailed answer.

Daisy sat down next to me and scrutinized my face. "We found him, Boo, so why aren't you smiling?"

"Because now we have to get him away from Tage."

"I'm guessing that won't be easy," Carter said.

No one had a response to that. My heart sank: now I knew where Maxwell was, but I didn't know how to help him. If I agreed to sell my soul, then Tage would probably let Maxwell go free. In fact, I realized, that must have been Tage's plan from the start. He'd win my soul even though Maxwell never really had been suffering in hell. All he had needed to do was make me think Maxwell was being tormented. Maybe he really was suffering, I thought. I didn't know how Maxwell had come to be imprisoned by Tage, but it must be taking a lot of force to keep him there. Maxwell was obviously unable to dematerialize from his prison, and I had no idea how a demon could be incapacitated like that.

Shaun was shaking his head. "How do you go up against a demon and win?"

"With a lot of faith and a lot of holy water," Lou answered.

Suddenly all eyes were on Lou. He was usually a wallflower, and he shifted uncomfortably at the sudden attention.

"You know how to fight a demon?" Daisy's voice was incredulous.

"In theory."

"How?" I asked.

"There are different ways, but the most common is to penetrate the demon's heart with an object that's been—"

"No, how do you know all this?" I interrupted.

"Oh. From studying." Lou's voice was confident, but he directed his answer toward the wall instead of me.

Lou's knowledge of demons and how to banish them was a relief, in our current situation, but his growing interest coincided a little too well with Maxwell's arrival in my life. I wasn't sure what that meant, but I didn't like it.

"Are you actually going to help us, then?" I hoped Lou would forgive my skepticism, but he had practically stopped speaking to me because of my relationship with Maxwell. Things had pretty much returned to normal after Maxwell's banishment—well, imprisonment—and I was surprised that Lou hadn't already washed his hands of this situation. Getting Maxwell back was definitely not something he would want.

But Lou surprised me. "Yes, for you."

I was so touched that I actually got up and hugged Lou. He reacted with his usual awkwardness, but I knew I sent the right message to him. This was a big sacrifice for Lou, and I appreciated it with every ounce of my being.

I sat back down feeling a little better. I hadn't expected that we had a secret weapon in our midst.

"If Lou knows how to deal with the demon," Carter said, "then how do we catch him off guard to help our chances? We can't just show up on his doorstep and ask if he can come out to play."

"That's exactly what we do," I said. "He won't see it coming."

"But then what? He opens the door, and Lou dumps holy water on him?" Shaun flashed a rueful smile.

"Tage is planning to come see me tomorrow so I can give him my decision. Maybe I knock on his door and tell him I couldn't wait to tell him. It won't explain how I got his address, but it should at least distract him from our real purpose."

"Give him your decision?" Lou said, confused.

"And why is Tage planning to see you tomorrow about it? Are you on a deadline?" Daisy chimed in.

It was surreal to think that of everyone in the room, only Carter knew the full story. I related it as quickly as I could to the others. Lou didn't even know about Tage's proposal to exchange my soul for Maxwell's freedom, and he was furious at the idea. If he had been harboring any doubts about banishing Tage, then he wasn't anymore. I'd never seen Lou's pale skin turn such a deep shade of red.

He could be dangerous if he got angry, I thought.

There was no telling what time Tage might pop up to see me on Sunday, and Shaun expressed concern over Tage showing up to find me not home. He might suspect something was going on.

"Then we need to leave as soon as possible," Daisy said.

"It's already after ten!" I protested.

Lou was shaking his head. "And I'm going to need time to prepare. I agree, though, that the sooner we leave, the better."

"We should arrive at dawn," Carter said.

"It's a four-hour drive to Atlanta," I argued. "We'd have to leave here at two a.m.! We'll have to take two cars since there are five of us, so that means two people have to drive all night on no sleep. Uh-uh, no. It's too dangerous."

"Betty, we're planning to go banish a demon, and you're worried about a little late-night driving?" Daisy gave me a playful shove.

"Well…" I began, but Carter cut me off.

"I think I have a solution to that. We'll take one car big enough for all of us. Let's plan to meet back here at two. Everyone go home and get whatever rest you can."

Shaun and Daisy agreed to take Carter back to Ron and Kerry's so he could retrieve his car. Within a few minutes, I was alone. I felt utterly exhausted by the night's events, but there was no way I could shut my brain down to sleep. Instead, I called out to Lieutenant Griffin. When he rattled the blinds in response to my call, I issued instructions.

"I need you to try to get a message to a ghost named Faith." I gave the Lieutenant Faith's address and described her using what details I knew. I had no idea if ghosts could actually see each other or not, but I figured it didn't hurt. "Tell everyone in your network to pass on the message. All you need to say is, 'We're coming.'"

The blind rattled once, which in Lieutenant Griffin speak meant 'yes.' He'd gotten the message. I hoped Faith would get it and somehow be able to relay it to Maxwell. If he had advance warning that we were coming, maybe there was something he could do from his end to help the rescue effort.

I spent the rest of my time sitting silently on the couch, staring blankly at my TV. I didn't even know what I was watching.

There was no point in arming myself with anything. A gun wouldn't kill Tage, nor would any other mundane weapon. I had to put my faith in Lou that he knew what he was doing. I showered—after all, if I was going to be crammed in a car with everyone for four hours, I didn't want to stink—dressed in jeans and a sweater, and put extra food and water out for Mina.

Daisy and Shaun arrived promptly at two, and Carter trailed in after them before I had shut my door. Lou finally showed up about fifteen minutes later, a harried but determined look on his face.

"Carter, you said we could take a car big enough for all of us. You bring your mom's mini-van?" I tried to smile to ward off the growing anxiety I felt.

"How can you joke when we have such a serious task ahead?" Carter said. "Of course I'm not driving anywhere in a mini-van. Let's go."

Everyone herded out the door. Before I followed, I stroked Mina on the head and whispered, "Let's hope I have Maxwell with me when I come back."

Carter had reprimanded me for making a joke, but when I walked out to the street I wondered if he was pulling a prank on us. There was a sleek black limousine parked at the curb. Daisy and Shaun were already climbing in the back while the driver, wearing a crisp black suit, held the door.

"You can't be serious," I said.

"Perfectly. What's the point in having connections if you don't use them?" Carter answered. "This way, none of us has to drive."

171

Carter motioned me ahead of him, and I was soon sinking into the black leather upholstery. When we were all inside and the driver shut the door, I said, "We're going to arrive at a demon's house in a limo. Only you, Carter." My laugh had a hysterical edge to it.

"It's better than a mini-van," he sniffed.

I had to agree with him there. We were quiet for much of the drive, and I nearly fell asleep as the limo glided through the vacant stretches of land between Savannah and Macon. When we got on the interstate that led north to Atlanta, though, my fears grew with every mile we covered.

I wasn't the only one feeling that way, and I had to admire my friends' loyalty. They had no stake in this fight: Maxwell was my boyfriend, and it was my soul that Tage was after. Still, every one of them had agreed to accompany me without question. No one had surprised me more than Lou, and I began to understand that he was looking forward to the upcoming confrontation. He had an odd gleam in his eyes.

It was still dark when we got to Atlanta, and Carter instructed the driver to pull over somewhere so we could wait for a while. We wanted to arrive at Tage's at dawn. I guess it didn't matter what time of day we went, but somehow it felt right to wait for the sun.

We wound up in an empty parking lot, and Shaun rolled down a tinted window to peep out every ten minutes. We didn't have to wait long before the sky began to lighten. Within half an hour, the eastern sky was orange and pink with the first rays of the sun.

Lou walked us through our plan again, which we had gone through many times already. It wasn't much of a plan, but it calmed all of our nerves a bit to hear Lou's confident voice.

We were going to our doom. At least that's how I felt

when the limo began to move again. I squeezed my eyes tightly shut and prayed as I never have before. Lou had reiterated the importance of faith in successfully banishing a demon. I wouldn't be wielding the holy water, but any faith I could muster might help.

We entered a quiet neighborhood of older houses that ranged from Victorian mansions to fifties-era bungalows. Huge oak trees shadowed the roads, and magnolia trees stood like sentries in front lawns. We turned onto Fifth, and I forgot to breathe.

The limo dropped us off a few houses down from number thirty-one. As we got out and huddled together on the sidewalk, I began to shiver from both the chill, damp air and the fear of what I was about to do.

"God watch over us and protect us, and guide our steps," Lou intoned.

I led the way, since Tage's business was with me. Daisy's firm hand on my back was the only thing propelling me forward. I couldn't feel my feet and nearly fell when I stumbled over a break in the old sidewalk.

Number thirty-one fit in so perfectly with the other houses in the neighborhood that no one would ever suspect a demon lived there. The single-story house was built in the Craftsman style of the early twentieth century, with a white façade and pale blue trim. The yard was elegantly kept, and a small fountain was bubbling away inside a ring of junipers.

I could hear the fountain and I could hear my heartbeat as I turned up the front walk, but all other noise in the world ceased. When I stepped up onto the front porch, my friends stayed behind on the walk. We had agreed that Tage would feel less threatened if we didn't crowd his doorstep. I wanted him to think I'd just brought along moral support.

I inhaled, breathed out a prayer, and rang the doorbell.

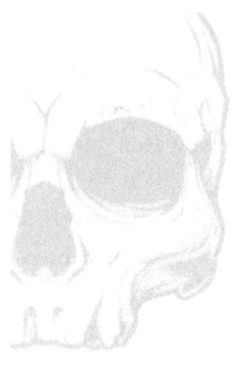

TWENTY-FOUR

I stood there for what seemed like hours, though in reality it couldn't have been more than half a minute. Tage answered the door, looking very human in nothing but black sweatpants. His eyes were bleary, and his hair stuck straight up.

When he saw me, his eyes cleared, and he snapped wide awake. "What are you doing here?"

"I came to give you my answer." My voice trembled, and Tage had to lean forward to hear me.

Tage's eyes narrowed. "I don't recall giving you my address."

"After you dropped in on me a few times, I thought the least I could do was return the favor."

Tage was silent.

"May I come in?" I asked.

Tage glanced behind him, and when he turned to the front again, he caught sight of my friends for the first time. "What's this, your cheering section?"

"I needed some moral support," I said.

Tage actually smiled at this. "So you've come to a decision, then?"

"Why else would I be here?"

"Let's hear it." Tage swept his hand in a grand gesture.

I bit my lip. Our plan was contingent on actually

getting inside Tage's house. If I gave him my answer now, there would be no need for me to go inside. I did the first thing I thought of. I pretended I was about to faint.

It wasn't that hard to do, actually. I had been up since the previous morning, and I had last eaten ten hours before. Those factors, combined with my fear and anxiety, had me feeling pretty woozy already. I fluttered my eyelids and relaxed my knees while I let my head droop forward. Tage himself caught me just as I reached out to grab the doorframe for balance.

"Come on, let's not put on a show for the early risers," he said, pulling me into the house. He was grinning now, enjoying my weakness.

"But…" I said, gesturing to the group on the lawn.

Tage sighed. "Fine, they can come, too, if you are that dependent on them."

Tage's warm arms felt smothering as he steered me down the hallway. I wanted to break free but had to maintain my act. Relief flooded through me when he eased me onto a low chair in his living room. Like Maxwell, Tage preferred antiques. Must be a demon thing, I mused.

Daisy, Shaun, and Carter sat on the couch while Lou stood to one side. Tage paced back and forth in front of me, creating a barrier between my friends and me. He addressed them first. "Welcome to my home. It's very nice of you to come witness Betty's downfall."

Daisy's eyes flashed, and she opened her mouth to retort, but a look from Shaun stopped her.

Turning to me, Tage said, "I have a bet going with another demon friend of mine. He says you'll never sell your soul for Maxwell, but I say otherwise. Tell me, Betty, which of us is correct? And be sure to answer clearly, so all your friends can hear."

Tage's face was triumphant. He obviously believed I was ready to sign the contract.

"My answer is no, I will not sell my soul." I said it loudly, drawing on all the faith and confidence I had in me.

"What?" Tage's smug smile quickly contorted into an expression of anger. "You stupid girl, I warned you not to say no to me." Before I could react, Tage lunged at me. His hands clamped around my shoulders, and he yanked me to my feet so that my face was inches from his. He spun me around so he could see both the others and me. When he spoke again, Tage's voice was quiet, which made it all the more menacing. "I will have your soul, however I have to get it. If you had given me the correct answer, I at least would have let you have Maxwell and live out your life."

"Where is Maxwell, anyway?" I asked. If I was going to die, I at least wanted some answers.

Tage just shook me and tightened his grip. "In my possession. But I'll banish him as soon as I'm done with you."

My arms grew warm from Tage's hands, and the heat began to radiate up into my shoulders and down into my hands. As the heat spread, it intensified and I felt pain welling up inside me. Tage was going to burn me alive. I'd seen Maxwell do it to other people, and I knew it would be an excruciating way to die. My tears only made Tage laugh.

It was the worst pain I'd ever felt in my life, like I'd been turned inside out and dropped in a pot of boiling water.

"I can make it stop, Betty." Tage's eyes were bright and hard, but his voice was light. "Agree to sell your soul to me, and I'll let you walk out of here alive."

I was in so much pain that it was hard to form words. It took all of my concentration to ask, "What about Maxwell?"

"You gave up your chance to save him. It's your own life you're bargaining for now." To emphasize his point, a wave of heat coursed through my body, the hottest and most intense I'd felt yet. I cried out from the pain while Tage smiled at me. "Give me your answer," he prompted.

As much pain as I was in, I knew that it was only temporary compared to the pain and suffering of hell. I had considered eternal anguish to save Maxwell from it, but a few minutes of Tage's torture here on Earth seemed like a better choice than hell. Besides, Tage had made it clear that nothing I did would save Maxwell. That was all up to the others now.

"No," I said. My voice was barely more than a whisper now. "You will never have my soul."

"An unfortunate choice, Betty," Tage said. "We could have been such friends, you and I." With that, the pain increased again. Red tinged my vision, slowly blotting out the scene before me.

Why hadn't Lou attacked Tage yet? I didn't know if he was frozen with fear or just waiting for the ideal moment. I heard Shaun shout, "He's killing her!"

My head lolled forward as my strength gave out. Tage's strong grip was the only thing keeping me on my feet. All I could see was red, all I could feel was pain, and all I could hear was Tage's exultant laugh. I'm going to die, I thought. But then a different thought broke through. A quiet voice seemed to tell me, "Have faith."

"I do," I whispered.

My words had no effect on Tage, but he suddenly looked down, and his laughing stopped abruptly. The heat began to subside, just enough so it was no longer painful. My vision cleared, and his face came into focus again.

"I can't kill you when you're wearing that," Tage said. He was eyeing the St. Michael medallion that Lou had given me. With one hand, Tage reached up and yanked the chain from my neck. He was careful not to touch the medallion itself, and he threw the chain away from him with a hiss.

The distraction gave Lou the opportunity to act. He lunged forward and reached out for me. "Betty, come here, get away from him!" he shouted.

Tage, of course, only held onto me more tightly. Lou had perfectly calculated his approach from the start: he knew if he went after Tage, the demon would back away. By trying to rescue me instead, Tage would stay close to keep his prize.

One of Tage's arms snaked around my shoulders, and he hugged me to him. He reached out to Lou with his other arm. "Stay back. When I'm finished killing her, I'll be more than happy to accommodate you, as well."

My face was pinned against Tage's shoulder, so I couldn't see what was happening. Tage's body shifted back and forth, as if he and Lou were taking turns lunging at each other. I gathered what strength I had and squirmed in Tage's grip, pushing against him with my hands while I twisted my torso.

Tage's attention returned to me momentarily. He shoved me onto the floor, and I fell face-first, narrowly missing the edge of a small table. Something warm and heavy pressed down on the back of my neck.

"Careful, friend, or I'll snap her neck before you can stop me," Tage warned.

Lou didn't say anything, but the pressure of Tage's foot against my neck relaxed, and I knew Lou was backing off.

Don't give up, Lou, I thought desperately.

Tage didn't move as the silence stretched. Finally, apparently satisfied that Lou wasn't going to attack again, Tage leaned down and said, almost kindly, "I do apologize for the interruption. Let's continue, shall we?"

Tage removed his foot from my neck, but before I

could move, I felt his hands against my back. The searing heat began to radiate from them again, and I moaned.

There was a noise somewhere else in the house, like a distant door slamming. Then I heard running and a breathless shout of, "Now!"

In an instant, Tage's entire body collapsed on top of me. The weight disappeared just as quickly, and all I felt was a sticky wetness on the back of my sweater.

Lou's voice was breathless. "Come on, Betty. It's okay."

I tentatively rolled over and looked up at Lou. He was sweating profusely, and there was a bloody knife in his hand. I didn't see Tage anywhere, but his sweatpants were in a heap on the floor beside me.

I grimaced as I craned my neck in an effort to peer at my back. "I lose more clothes to demon blood," I mumbled. I wasn't sure I could stand yet, so I stretched my arms out to Lou. He kneeled down and let me hug him.

"You did it?" I asked.

Lou nodded. "You should have seen the look on his face. I'll be having nightmares about that for weeks."

I laughed weakly and hugged Lou harder. "Come on," he said. "They found Maxwell."

Those were probably the only words that could have gotten me to my feet. Carter was the one who had run into the room and shouted. While Tage had been busy with Lou and me, the others had gone through the house to search for Maxwell. We didn't want to banish Tage until we knew where Maxwell was, and Carter's shout had been Lou's signal to banish as he pleased.

Carter and Lou gingerly helped me to my feet. I was unsteady but was at least able to follow them down the hall without assistance. Carter led us through a small door at the rear of the hallway and down a set of rickety wooden steps into the basement.

There was just one dim light bulb illuminating the

scene, but I could see Daisy crouched down next to a wooden crate about the size of an armchair. She had her hand held up to a gap between the slats, and her fingers were holding tightly to someone else's. I heard Daisy say, "Here she is. She's okay." I was already stumbling down the last few steps in my haste.

I sank down next to Daisy, and she relinquished Maxwell's hand to me. His fingers felt clammy, instead of their usual overly-warm temperature. I put my face up to the crate, straining to see him in the darkness inside.

"Maxwell, are you all right?"

"I will be now," Maxwell said. His voice was weak, and I thought he might be crying. I knew I was.

Shaun had been scouring the basement and found a long screwdriver to pry open the top of the crate. It came off easily, and I was surprised that such a trivial cage had been able to keep Maxwell imprisoned.

Until, at least, I saw Maxwell. I released his hand so I could stand up and peer inside the crate. Maxwell was slumped against one side, his face a flat shade of gray underneath his dark beard. His brilliant blue eyes were dulled, and his breathing was shallow.

He was also dirty and dressed in a ratty pair of sweat-pants and a tee-shirt, which for Maxwell was probably as bad as being locked in a crate.

I stood by helplessly while Shaun and Carter grabbed Maxwell underneath the arms and hauled him up and out of the crate. He sank down onto the dirt floor of the basement, and I knelt beside him.

"Maxwell," I said, but I didn't know what else to say. I was elated to see him alive and to know that he was safe. At the same time, it broke my heart to see how weak and ill he was, and I worried that Tage might have injured him permanently.

"Betty," Maxwell whispered. He took my hand and

brought it up to his cracked lips. He closed his eyes and sighed.

"Can someone get him a glass of water?" I said.

Maxwell didn't move or speak until Daisy returned from the kitchen with a glass of water. He drank deeply and gave me a small smile. "I will be all right," he assured.

"What did Tage do to you?" I was so used to Maxwell being strong and resilient, and it scared me to see him in his current state. I guess I'd expected him to just pop out of the crate unharmed.

Instead of answering, Maxwell turned his left arm up. The inside of his elbow was covered in pinpricks.

"Injections?" I asked.

"Just enough holy water to keep me incapacitated," Maxwell said. "Sometimes I hoped he'd give me too much, and I'd be banished. I think it would have hurt less." Maxwell paused, then added, "I also haven't eaten since I got here."

Demons are immortal, and there are only a few ways to successfully banish one. I couldn't imagine how awful starvation must be when there would be no death as a release.

Daisy promised to get something for Maxwell while Carter and Shaun helped him up and out of the house. With Tage banished, and a very conspicuous limo parked down the street, we knew we ought to leave before we turned too many heads.

Soon we were on the road and on the way back home. Daisy had climbed in the limo with a bowl of dry cereal. She insisted that Maxwell needed to eat just a little of something bland since he hadn't had food for two weeks. "And Tage won't miss the bowl," she said with a shrug.

Maxwell sat next to me in the very back of the limo. The walk and a little fresh air had revived him a fraction, and he looked less sickly already. He picked at his cereal with one hand while keeping the other clamped over mine. While he ate, we told him about the bizarre clues Faith had left for us, Tage's deal for my soul, and our eventual rescue mission. Maxwell gave a bittersweet smile when Lou described Tage's banishment. "He was a good friend of mine for many years," Maxwell said.

"He wasn't a good friend for the past two weeks," Daisy reminded him.

Maxwell just nodded in agreement.

"I really believed you'd been banished," I said quietly. "That demon hunter…"

"He didn't hurt you, did he?"

"No. I think he felt sorry for me."

Maxwell leaned over and kissed me softly, then laid his head on my shoulder. "I'm so sorry I had to let you believe I'd been banished. I meant to come back later that night, but…" Maxwell fell silent.

Soon I heard Maxwell's soft, regular breathing. I kissed the top of his head and closed my eyes. I was asleep in minutes, comforted by the growing warmth in Maxwell's fingers.

When I finally woke up, Daisy was pushing a bag of fast food into my hands. "You haven't eaten in hours, Boo, and you had a rough morning of it," she was saying. Everyone else, including Maxwell, was already awake.

"Are we home?" I rubbed my eyes and yawned.

"We're about an hour away. Here, eat."

I took the bag from Daisy and did as she said. It was the best meal I'd ever tasted in my life.

With all of us awake and feeling at least somewhat better, Maxwell sighed and gave me a significant look. "I guess it's time for me to tell my side of the story," he said.

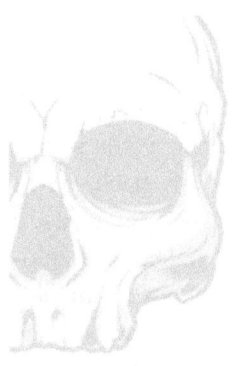

TWENTY-FIVE

"I didn't know what to do when that demon hunter appeared at the party," Maxwell began. "The only thought I had was that I needed to draw his attention away from you, Betty. If I'd had time to think of a plan before he attacked, I would have told you. I hated knowing that you believed I was banished.

"As it was, I had to come up with something while I ran from him. I've seen demons banished before and know they just disappear. So, I thought, if I dematerialized at the right time, it would appear that I'd been banished. The demon hunters could cross me off their list, and you and I both would be out of danger, at least until they realized their mistake. It seemed perfect.

"I looked over my shoulder and waited for the hunter to shoot his arrow. I knew I had to time it perfectly. I nearly waited too long. It wasn't until I materialized at Tage's house that I realized the tip of the arrow had pierced my skin."

"Why did you go to Tage's?" Carter interrupted. "He seemed like a creep."

Maxwell laughed quietly. "He was, but he'd also been a good friend to me over the years. I thought I'd just lay low at his place for a bit, then pop back over to Savannah later that night. I didn't want Betty to wait too long before I returned."

"How did you wind up in a crate?" I asked.

"Tage was surprised to see me, especially in the state I was in. The arrow had barely penetrated my back, but it was enough to severely weaken me. Materializing at Tage's took everything I had left. So there I was, naked and helpless in the middle of Tage's living room." Maxwell laughed sardonically. "He gave me some clothes and helped me onto the couch, and I told him what had happened. Tage has heard your name before, Betty, but I don't think he realized until that night how important you are to me. While we were talking, he got this really odd look on his face. I've known the guy for a hundred and fifty years, and I knew that look meant trouble. Nothing came of it at first, though, and later when he got me a glass of water, I didn't think anything of it. I drank half the glass before I started feeling its effects and knew it was laced with holy water."

"Wait a minute," Daisy interjected, her hand raised like she was in school. "Why would a demon have holy water on hand?"

Maxwell shrugged. "For protection against other demons, maybe. I've heard of some who ingest a little every day in an effort to build up immunity. It never turns out well. I'm guessing Tage had made some enemies and wanted to be ready if he was ever attacked."

"He definitely wasn't immune to holy water or to blessed objects. Betty's medallion gave him some trouble," Lou said.

I sat up straight and clutched at the area where the medallion should have been. "My necklace! I lost it!"

Lou just chuckled softly and reached into his pocket. When he withdrew his hand, my necklace was dangling from his fingers. "I picked it up before we left."

The clasp had broken when Tage tore the chain from

my neck, but I gratefully put it in my pocket. "Best present ever, Lou," I said.

"So he just gave you a holy water roofie and stuck you in a box?" Carter asked, turning his attention to Maxwell.

"Pretty much. I was nearly unconscious and in more pain than I can describe, so I couldn't put up a fight. Tage tied me up in his basement that first night, but then he brought that crate in and kept me in there. In my state, I couldn't have escaped, anyway. I think the crate was just his way of reminding me that I was his prisoner."

"When did he tell you that he was trying to trade your life for my soul?" I felt Maxwell's fingers tighten at the mention.

"Immediately. He couldn't wait to brag about his plan. After his visits to you, he'd come back and tell me about your reaction, and how upset you were at the idea of me being in torment. He felt sure that you'd give up your soul for me." Maxwell's eyes locked on Carter's. "Though he briefly doubted his chance of success when he found you at Betty's one night."

"He thought I was trying to talk her out of it?" Carter's voice was mockingly innocent.

"He thought you two were together." Maxwell was glaring now.

Carter smiled mischievously, almost daring Maxwell to ask the question that was on his lips. I rolled my eyes. "Stop it," I said, addressing them both. "Tage would have known better if he'd done his homework. It's bad enough that I had to convince someone at work that I wasn't involved with Tage." I shuddered.

Carter screwed up his face in disgust. "Yuck. I should hope your taste is better than that. His wardrobe, Betty…" He trailed off, apparently too horrified by the thought of ratty tee-shirts to continue.

"Sorry," Maxwell mumbled, loud enough only for me to hear. "Two weeks in a cage can make a guy a little nuts."

"You do know I'd never, ever date Carter, right?" I said, my voice just as low.

Maxwell's eyes flicked toward Carter. "Yes, I do now. At Tage's, though, I started to lose hope in everything. I was too vulnerable to hear what he told me without being affected."

"Never lose hope," I whispered. "Besides," I added, raising my voice, "I'm sure some of what Tage told you was exaggerated."

Daisy leaned forward before Maxwell could reply. "Let's talk about Faith."

"I owe her a huge debt," Maxwell said. "Tage's house is haunted; I learned that the first night when I kept hearing crying there in the basement. It was a woman, though I never saw her or learned her story. I knew that if she could get a message to a ghost in Savannah, then I might be able to reach someone."

"How did you wind up communicating through Faith?" Shaun asked. "We know you lived at her house once, but she died before you ever got there."

"Faith was a friendly companion when I lived in that house. I bought her some toys, and she was content to remain there with me rather than crossing over. It's the closest I've ever been to fatherhood." Maxwell smiled fondly, his eyes unfocused and distant. It was a few moments before he continued. "I knew Faith was still there. Sometimes I'll walk past that house, and she'll come right out to the front steps to greet me. If any ghost in Savannah was going to help me, I knew it would be Faith.

"I started giving messages to the ghost in Tage's basement. I had no idea if she heard or understood me, but I persisted. I nearly went hoarse from repeating my messages over and over. Whenever Tage was gone, I was talking."

"You never knew we received the messages?" I couldn't imagine being in Maxwell's situation, persisting in sending calls for help that might never be received.

"Not until last night. There was a little window at the top of one of the basement walls, and it had blinds over it. I woke up in the middle of the night, and the blinds were banging. It was the first time the ghost had done anything other than cry, so I suspected she was trying to tell me something. I tried asking questions, but she just continued to bang on the blinds. There's only one ghost I know who regularly communicates that way."

"Lieutenant Griffin. I asked him to get the word out that we were coming." My Spirit Sentry was more valuable than I had realized.

"It wasn't much to go by, but it gave me some hope. I was still surprised, though, when I heard the doorbell ring this morning. I couldn't hear enough to know what was going on until Carter, Shaun, and Daisy came running down the stairs. I've never been so happy to see familiar faces in my life, but it scared me that yours wasn't among them, Betty."

"I was dealing with other obstacles." I poked a finger against my stomach. "I'd say I'm medium, medium-well now."

"You're joking now, but it must have hurt. Even I've never been on the receiving end of an incineration."

"You don't want to be. It was awful, and that's all I'm going to say about it. I'm hoping my brain will conveniently lose that entire memory."

Maxwell just sighed in response and drew me closer to him.

I hadn't been paying attention to the scene outside our windows, but when we came to a stop, I looked out. The interstate had given way to the streets of Savannah, and I was nearly home. Not only that, but we were all safe, and Maxwell was by my side.

The noon bells were just ringing out from the cathedral when the limo stopped in front of my carriage house. We had been gone for less than twelve hours.

We all alighted, but Carter had only done so to say good-bye. He was going home in the limo, and we all thanked him for the wonderfully convenient—if slightly absurd—transportation arrangements. I hugged Carter and promised to talk to him soon. He might be an arrogant jerk most of the time, but he was proving to be a loyal friend. I decided that he and I might get along just fine, after all, as long as we didn't spend too much time together.

Daisy declared that she could in no way wait to get to her house before using the bathroom, so I handed her the key to my front door before I hugged Lou. "Thank you, Lou," I said. The words felt completely inadequate. Lou hated the fact that I dated a demon, but he'd risked his own life to save Maxwell. And, in the process, Lou had banished a demon. He would have the nightmares for weeks, but I knew Lou was proud of what he'd done. I suspected he'd wanted to try his hand at demon hunting for a while, and Maxwell's imprisonment had been the perfect excuse for Lou to jump into action. How long he had been studying to be a hunter, I didn't know. Lou's heightened interest in theology coupled with his aversion to Maxwell had made me suspicious, but I hadn't expected Lou to be quite so enthusiastic about banishing. I wondered how much bounty he'd collect on Tage.

I also wondered who would be next on his list.

My dark thoughts flitted through my mind in seconds, and I hugged Lou again to make them go away. He was still my friend, and I knew that no matter whom I dated,

Lou had my best interests at heart. Lou cared about me; that hadn't changed.

I turned to head into my apartment. Daisy and Shaun were already inside, and Maxwell walked gingerly beside me. He was still weak, but at least he didn't need assistance anymore.

My hand was on the doorknob when Lou cleared his throat behind me. "Uh, Maxwell, a word, please?"

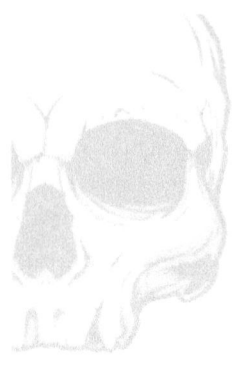

TWENTY-SIX

My hand froze. What could Lou possibly have to say to Maxwell? I wanted to turn around and join them so I could hear the conversation. No, I told myself, I have to trust Lou. I forced myself to turn the doorknob, and I reluctantly shut the door behind me so they could speak privately.

My anxiety must have shown on my face, because as soon as Daisy emerged from my bathroom—looking vastly relieved—she frowned at me. "What?" she said.

I told her that Lou and Maxwell were outside talking.

"Lou wouldn't do anything to hurt you, Betty."

"It's not me I'm worried about."

"No, I mean, he wouldn't hurt Maxwell as long as he makes you happy. If that changes, then Lou won't have anything to hold him back."

I'd been miserable when I thought Maxwell had been banished. If he were banished by Lou, I'd feel even worse. My breath came out in a huff. "Let's hope Maxwell keeps making me happy, then."

Maxwell came in soon after. He was silent, but he didn't look upset, so I took that as a good sign. Daisy and Shaun took his entrance as their cue to leave, but not before Daisy hugged Maxwell so violently that I thought he might collapse. She also admonished him to continue eating small portions of bland food until he had recovered.

I rounded on Maxwell as soon as the door was closed. "What did Lou say?"

Maxwell gestured vaguely. "Your friends care about you a great deal, Betty."

"He threatened you, didn't he?"

"Let's just say that I don't ever want to be on the wrong side of Lou and a blessed knife."

"I'm sorry. I knew he was anti-demon, but until last night I didn't know just how much."

"He has every right to be." Maxwell folded me into his arms, and I could feel some of his strength returning. "Besides, he helped save my life and yours this morning. I'm willing to take a few threats for that."

"Is it time for bed?" I asked.

"It's time for a hot shower." Maxwell's fingers plucked at the back of my sweater. "For both of us."

The demon blood on my sweater had dried to a crusty brown, and I took it off carefully to keep it from flaking all over my bedroom floor. Another good piece of clothing ruined. An awful lot of my wardrobe had wound up in the trashcan since I met Maxwell.

I put on the most comfortable, least sexy pajamas I owned after I showered. Part of my brain argued that I ought to be wearing something risqué since Maxwell was finally back, but sleep was my only priority now that he was safe. Plus, I didn't really own anything risqué.

Maxwell emerged from the bathroom in the tee and pajama pants he had left at my apartment a few weeks ago. Even when I'd thought he was gone forever, I hadn't had the heart to throw them out.

"You're looking better," I said.

"I'm feeling better. It's going to take a while for the

holy water to work its way out of my system, but I should be back to normal within a couple of days."

Maxwell stretched out on my bed, his eyes gazing at the ceiling.

"Would you rather sleep in your own bed tonight? You haven't seen it in a while."

"I'm happy to sleep wherever you are. Besides, now that I'm finally lying down, I don't think I could get up if I tried."

My blinds couldn't keep all the sunshine out, but it didn't matter. Maxwell was already asleep by the time I turned off my bedroom light and slid under the covers next to him.

When I woke up at eight o'clock that night, I was starving. I suspected that Maxwell felt the same way: he was already up and eating a stack of crackers.

"I'm trying to do as Nurse Daisy says," he said in greeting.

"Well, I'm ordering Chinese because I don't have the energy to cook." Out of habit, I also made a pot of coffee. It just seemed abnormal to get out of bed and not make coffee, even though it might keep me awake later.

Maxwell couldn't resist eating some of my noodles once my food arrived, and I think the food did him some good. He sat up straighter after he ate, and his face regained most of its normal coloring.

While we ate, Maxwell asked me what had been going on in my life for the past two weeks. I filled him in on the haunted house investigation, Carter's sudden agreeable attitude, and Daisy's new job.

"He's up to something," Maxwell said.

"I think so, too. No one just changes like that overnight. But it helped Daisy get a good job, so who am I to complain?"

"Just be wary, Betty."

I thought I could still detect a hint of jealousy in Maxwell's voice, and I smiled mysteriously. "What's wrong? Worried I'm going to leave you for a well-bred Southern gentleman?"

Maxwell laughed. "No. I know better than to think you'd ever go for Carter. Like I said, I was willing to entertain some pretty dark thoughts inside that crate, but now that I'm free and rational once again, I'm not worried."

After dinner, I returned to my bedroom to retrieve Maxwell's phone, car keys, and driver's license. The bullet remained hidden in my jewelry box. "Tage told me to burn everything," I explained, passing the items to Maxwell. "But I knew your keys and phone wouldn't burn."

"My license would have melted," Maxwell said.

"It has your picture on it. I couldn't burn it."

"Tomorrow I'll charge my phone and see how many voicemails are waiting. I'm going to have a lot of explaining to do."

"Can't you just claim a relative was sick and you had to leave town unexpectedly?"

"It will be something along those lines. Still, two weeks is no excuse for being out of touch. Maybe I can claim I hit my head and forgot who I was for a while."

Maxwell suddenly turned to me and put his hand against my cheek. "I nearly did, you know. If I'd stayed in that crate much longer, I think I would have forgotten who I was. Pain and confinement really can drive a man to madness."

"You wouldn't have been in there much longer, anyway. Tage was going to banish you because I told him I wasn't going to sell my soul."

"Betty…" Maxwell paused and looked at me carefully. "If my messages hadn't gotten through to you, and you had gone on believing I was banished to hell, what would you have told Tage?"

"I don't know. We did get your messages, so it never had to come to that point."

"You must have had some idea of what your decision would have been."

I looked at Maxwell steadily. "I'll never tell," I said.

Maxwell looked like he wanted to argue, but he remained silent. He stroked my face then bent forward and kissed me deeply. I giggled.

"Sorry," I said, pulling back just an inch. "Your beard tickles!"

Maxwell took that as his cue to kiss me more, and he took great pleasure in kissing me all over my neck and earlobes in an attempt to find which spot was the most ticklish.

We stayed up late, not talking much but enjoying being in each other's company again. Despite sleeping all afternoon, we were both still tired. I slept until my alarm clock reminded me that it was Monday morning and I had to go to work. I got out of bed reluctantly, wishing I could remain entwined with Maxwell instead.

Maxwell was definitely looking better, and he breathed deeply after he woke. "I almost feel like a real demon again," he said, stretching. He wasn't sure, however, if he could materialize yet. Instead, I dropped him off at his house on my way to work. Maxwell kissed me before he got out of the car, leaving me with a promise to shave off his beard before I saw him again.

After work, through which I trudged to the best of my ability, Maxwell called to propose we take a walk. His voice sounded odd, and I had no idea what he was planning. I would find out, he promised, when I got to his house.

My breath rushed out when Maxwell opened his front door. He looked completely recovered: his clean-shaven face was as pale and smooth as ever, his blue eyes shone, and his black hair had been trimmed and restored to its "just got out of bed" look. He was also wearing a three-piece black suit with a gray shirt.

Had Maxwell always been this handsome? I had forgotten how gorgeous he was in the two weeks since I'd last seen him in this state. I suddenly remembered a painting I'd once seen on a school field trip. It had been the most beautiful painting I'd ever seen, but when I got home and tried to describe it to my parents, I couldn't quite remember what it had looked like. Maxwell was like that painting: too perfect for my imperfect memory.

Instead of saying any of that, though, I only managed a quiet, "Hi."

Maybe my expression was doing a better job communicating, because Maxwell just pulled me into his arms and kissed me. He held me for a long time without saying a word. Eventually, he pulled back and looked at me a little sadly. "I missed you so much," he said.

Instead of inviting me inside, Maxwell locked up and walked me down to the sidewalk, where he offered his arm. "Shall we?"

I slid my arm though his. "Shall we what?"

"I told you we were taking a walk." So he was still being mysterious.

We strolled slowly, talking quietly while I snuggled up against Maxwell's side. It wasn't until we rounded a corner that I knew where we were going.

"Oh, no," I said, stopping. "Carla Jensen does not want me showing up on her doorstep."

"But she's expecting you. I got her number from Daisy and had a chat with her earlier."

I eyed Maxwell. "What are you planning to do?"

"I'm just dropping in to say hello to Faith."

Despite Maxwell's reassurances that I would actually be welcome in the Jensen household, I was still nervous while we stood at their front door. Carla and Scott stood next to each other when the door opened. Scott was smiling, but Carla still looked wary.

This was Maxwell's visit, so after I said hello I let him do the talking. Once we were seated in the living room, he said, "Like I said on the phone to Carla, I went to Atlanta for my business and wound up slipping on a wet stair. I woke up in the hospital and was too confused to go anywhere for a while or to even remember very much. Apparently I hit my head really hard when I fell."

The excuse sounded ridiculous to my ears, but then, I guess, the truth would sound even more outrageous. Besides, with Maxwell's charm and smooth delivery, I think Carla would have believed him even if he'd said that aliens had abducted him.

"Apparently I mumbled in my sleep a lot, and the doctors kept asking me who Betty was. I couldn't remember and, unfortunately, I'd lost my phone during my little adventure. I knew I was from Savannah because it said so on my driver's license, so I figured this Betty must be, too. The only problem was finding a way to get in touch with her.

"My hospital room was haunted, so I asked the ghost to get the word out to other spirits in Savannah. I wanted to let Betty know I was okay, but I needed help. I had little else to relay but hoped it would be enough."

"Well, we're certainly glad to see you've recovered," Scott said. "You remember everything now, I suppose?"

"I don't remember the fall, and there are long stretches of my time in Atlanta that are lost to me," Maxwell lied smoothly. "But I do remember everything before I went to Atlanta."

"Our house was in an uproar thanks to you," Carla said. She was clearly not over her own trauma, and I couldn't really blame her.

"I heard about what happened here. Please, at least

allow me to pay for new furniture in your bedrooms to replace what got ruined."

Carla's eyes lit up, and I think she was on the verge of agreeing when Scott said, "Thank you, but there's no need. Most of the furniture we can repaint. It will take some time but won't be expensive."

"Have you had any activity lately?" I asked.

Carla shook her head. "It's back to normal around here, like nothing ever happened. Faith calmed down sometime Saturday night, and now she's back to her usual: playing with the boys' toys when no one is looking, and wandering around upstairs."

"I guess she got the message that everything was okay," Maxwell said.

Now that he had addressed the family, Maxwell asked if he could go talk to Faith. Carla and Scott agreed to give us some time with her, and we went upstairs to visit her in Derek's room.

"She was in the living room with us, you know," Maxwell whispered as we walked upstairs. "I didn't say anything because I wanted to speak with her privately."

I hadn't seen anything, and Derek's room was void of any ghostly girls when we walked in. Or so I thought, at least. The mattress suddenly dipped and rose several times. Maxwell laughed. "She's jumping on the bed." He claimed he could see Faith, with her blonde curls and crisp white dress. It must have been some demonic ability, because once she stopped jumping on the bed, the only evidence I had of Faith's presence was the raised hair on my arms.

"It's good to see you, Faith," Maxwell said quietly. "You saved my life." Maxwell told her a simplified version of what had happened to him and how Faith's help had allowed us to rescue him. "Thank you so much, Faith," Maxwell concluded. "I owe you a great debt."

Maxwell listened to the little voice I couldn't hear. "I

miss you, too," he answered. After another pause, he said, "Yes, she's a very nice lady. I'll tell her you said so."

I leaned forward and addressed the empty space where Maxwell seemed to be looking. "Thank you for your help, Faith," I said. "If you ever need our help, just get the message to Lieutenant Griffin. He lives with me, and he's very nice."

"She says, 'You're welcome,'" Maxwell relayed. "Faith, I'll see you soon. Goodbye."

"Bye, Faith," I said, waving.

When we returned to the living room, Maxwell shook hands with both Scott and Carla. "She's very happy here," he said. "She says she likes all the toys in the house, and she's glad that you make her feel like a part of the family."

"Tell her we're glad to have her," Scott said.

"As long as she's not ruining the walls and furniture!" Carla added.

Maxwell smiled. "You should tell her yourself. When you feel like she's present, talk to her like you would to anyone else. The attention means a lot to her."

Once we were outside again, I took Maxwell's arm as I had done on the way over. He put his hand over mine and sighed. He looked sad and introspective.

"You should be happy that all of this is over," I said.

"I am."

"You don't look like it. Are you still feeling the effects of the holy water?"

"I'm fully recovered, or close to it. I haven't tried to materialize anywhere yet, but I haven't had any need to."

I let the subject drop, and we were silent for a time. The sound of nearby church bells chiming the hour brought Maxwell out of his reverie. "Here I was so worried about a demon hunter hurting you that I never even considered that another demon might be a threat," he said.

"A friend of yours, no less."

"And if a friend of mine would do such an awful thing, what might a demon who's not my friend do? Betty, despite my best efforts, you're just not safe with me."

"You've made that clear in the past, but you know it's a risk I'm willing to take."

Maxwell stopped walking and turned to me. "It's not a risk I'm willing to take."

I suddenly felt cold, despite Maxwell's warm hand over mine. I wanted to hold onto him, to tell him I wasn't going anywhere, but I recognized the determined look in his eyes. He was going to leave me because he thought it would protect me. "Please, Maxwell," I whispered.

"I love you, Betty. I don't want any more harm to come to you. What if Faith hadn't gotten her message through? Your soul might belong to hell by now. Or what if Lou hadn't been able to banish Tage? It takes a lot of spiritual strength to do such a thing, and if he had faltered, you would have been killed. I would have gotten out of that prison to find only your ashes. I can't take that risk. I'd rather give you up than risk losing you. I wouldn't be able to live with myself if something happened to you, and it was all my fault."

Maxwell's words were bittersweet. I felt a soaring delight when he said he loved me, but the rest of his words chipped away at my joy until I felt hollow inside.

"I love you, too, Maxwell, and if something did happen to me, at least I'd die happy because I had you."

"You don't need me to be happy." Maxwell's voice was sad. "After a while, you'll probably realize you're a lot happier without me."

"How can you say that?"

"Because I've caused you nothing but trouble."

"That's not true." I could feel anger beginning to well up inside me, and my voice rose. "You saved my life from those lowlifes that Mr. Stiles hired to kill me. Twice, in fact."

"Yes," Maxwell agreed, "I kept you alive only to put your life and your soul in mortal danger. You were right when you broke up with me before. I'm a demon, Betty. Even if I'm not trying to cause chaos in your life, it's still going to happen, no matter how much I wish it were otherwise."

"One friend betrayed you, and now you're going to break up with me?"

"One friend betrayed me, one demon hunter tried to kill me, and you could have been hurt—or worse—on both occasions. Once word gets out that I'm still alive, more hunters will come after me, and other demons will see an opportunity to exploit your feelings for me. It won't stop. Ever."

I opened my mouth to protest. Couldn't Maxwell understand that I was willing to face any kind of danger for him? If I had to stave off a demon hunter every week, I would do it to keep him safe. I'd dealt with demons before, and would gladly do it again, as long as Maxwell was by my side.

I realized then that Maxwell did, in fact, understand. He knew I would risk everything, even my soul, for him, and that was the problem. Maxwell knew I was willing to make sacrifices for him, and he was terrified I'd wind up sacrificing myself. I remembered how much I'd struggled with the choice Tage had given me: to sell my soul or to refuse and go on living with the knowledge that Maxwell was banished. It would be like that for Maxwell if something happened to me: he would have to go on living his immortal existence, knowing I'd died because of him.

There had been times during Maxwell's long years that he had gleefully led people to their deaths; he'd even bragged about it to me. But looking at his face now, at the despair and fear that lined his forehead, I knew it was different this time. Maxwell really did love me, and he couldn't bear to lose me.

I shut my eyes. I knew I would cry later, but right now I didn't want to make this any harder for Maxwell. "I'm going to miss you so much," I whispered.

When I opened my eyes again, a tear was sliding down Maxwell's pale cheek.

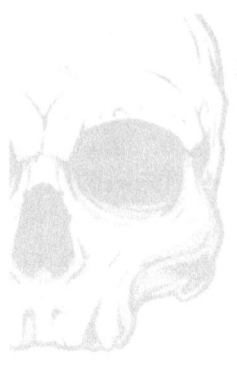

TWENTY-SEVEN

I think Maxwell was surprised by my compliance. He knew me well enough to expect stubborn resistance, and as he walked me back to my car in front of his house, I tried to explain to him that I understood why he was leaving me.

Of course, that didn't make it hurt any less when he said goodbye. Maxwell kissed me so hard that I bent backwards to try to escape the force of his lips, but he wrapped his arms around me tighter so that I couldn't move. As I felt his strong back under my hands for the last time, I wished fervently that he would never let me go.

Eventually, though, he did.

I soaked up one last view of Maxwell, looking into those beautiful blue eyes that I would never see again. There were no words, just a look between us.

I didn't start crying until long after I'd gotten home. Daisy came over as soon as I called her, and she cried right along with me.

Sleep didn't come for a long time that night, and I listened to the muffled sounds of the city around me, wondering if I would see Maxwell again. It was easy to think that our breaking up meant we'd never see each other, but Savannah's historic district was like living in a small town. Chances were good that we'd run into each other down on River Street, stroll through the same square, or even pull up to the same intersection at the same time.

Then again, I reminded myself, I'd never seen Maxwell before we'd met just over a month before. I could never have seen that face and forgotten it, even if he'd been a stranger to me.

I also wasn't sure that I wanted to see Maxwell again. Perhaps, in time, I could handle it, but to see him now, when I knew I couldn't have him and the pain was so fresh, would be too hard. It was also possible that he didn't want to see me anytime in the near future and would take steps to make sure we didn't meet accidentally.

The rest of my week was a fuzzy blur. I went to work, I ate, I slept, but I did it all like someone in a dream. I'd grieved when I'd thought Maxwell had been banished, I'd worried when I learned he was Tage's prisoner, I'd rejoiced when he was by my side again, and I'd cried when he terminated our relationship. It was too many emotions in too short a time.

Daisy and Shaun made me go to The Burglar Bar with them on Wednesday night, insisting that I needed to get out of the house. It only made me feel worse, trying to eat dinner at the same table where I'd first met Maxwell.

My phone rang on Thursday, and I answered it without even glancing at the caller I.D. I was expecting Daisy to call and check up on me, as she had every day since Monday. Instead, I was surprised to hear Carter's voice.

"How are you, Betty?" By his tone, he clearly knew the answer already.

"Surviving."

"I ran into Daisy at Dad's office. She told me."

"I saw the Jensens, and they said Faith is back to her usual quiet behavior," I said, changing the subject.

"Which is your way of saying you don't want to talk about it."

"Of course I don't want to talk about it," I snapped, stopping myself before I added, "with you." Carter and I might be forming a tenuous friendship, but that didn't mean I was ready to cry on his shoulder. "Sorry, Carter. I'm just…not right."

"Daisy's worried that you might hide in your apartment and become some depressed little hermit."

"I'm considering it."

"I've got an alternative for you. I'm going to a Halloween party Saturday night. I think you should go with me. It would be good for you to get out, meet some new people."

I frowned. "What kind of Halloween party?"

"A masquerade. So, a nice dress and a mask. It doesn't even require that much effort on your part. Come on, Betty."

"Okay, I'll go, but only because I suspect you're plotting with Daisy, which means that if I turn you down, I'll get a lecture from her."

"Good girl. I promise you'll have fun." Carter hung up, and I realized that I needed yet another nice dress for yet another nice Halloween party. Except this time, it wasn't with the date of my dreams.

———— ✦ ————

When Carter arrived to pick me up on Saturday, I was wearing a simple black dress with an empire waist. The skirt flowed in gauzy layers down to my knees, and I had on black stockings and heels. Picking out this dress had been much easier than shopping for my date with Maxwell: I wasn't nearly as concerned about looking good as I had been three weeks before. And, of course, Daisy had enthusiastically gone to the mall with me on Friday night.

The mask I'd found was black with silver trim and a spray of black feathers along the top. It was attached to a satin-covered stick, which meant I didn't have to actually wear it. Since I would be putting the mask up to my face, I kept my hair simple, curling it under a little at the ends so it perfectly framed my face.

I had hardly looked at myself in the mirror, so I was surprised when I opened the door and heard a soft, "Wow." Carter was a hard man to impress, and I had expected him to have something negative to say about my wardrobe choice.

And, I had to admit, Carter looked really good. He was a portrait of Southern gentility, wearing a tuxedo that fit him perfectly. No rentals for him, I thought. This tux was obviously tailored to his tall, haughty form, and nothing could have suited him better. Not one of his blonde hairs was out of place.

"I didn't realize this was such a formal party," I said, self-consciously smoothing my dress.

"You have nothing to worry about," Carter assured me.

The party was a charity fundraiser, and some prominent Savannah family had offered their home for the event. By home, they meant giant plantation house on the outskirts of town. The two-story house was illuminated with blue spotlights that cast a spooky glow across the backyard. A few people mingled inside, but most were on the back lawn, enjoying the mild weather and a small orchestra playing on a portable stage.

Carter offered his arm when we got out of his car, and I was painfully reminded of Maxwell making the same gesture right before he broke up with me. I brought my mask up to my face, hoping it would hide whatever might be showing there. Carter had a black leather mask with a single red stripe that ran like a teardrop down one cheek.

It felt strange to walk into the party on Carter's arm. It was so formal that it reminded me of a date. Less than a week after Maxwell broke up with you, I thought, and here you are at a party with another man.

But that's exactly why I'm here, I realized. Carter was being kind enough to try to cheer me up, and the least I could do was attempt to enjoy myself.

Carter knew a lot of the people there, and when he made introductions, I recognized names from some of the oldest families in Savannah. Not once did Carter make me feel inferior, though I knew that I fell far short in comparison to the rank and money that was all around me.

After Carter made his rounds, the orchestra began playing a slow song, and a few couples started dancing in front of the stage.

"Would you like to dance?" Carter held out his hand. "I normally hate it, but I'll make an exception for you."

"All right." I put my hand into Carter's, and he led me onto the dance floor. As we danced, I felt someone's eyes on me. I looked over Carter's shoulder and saw a pair of intense blue eyes staring at me from behind an intricate mask in the shape of a raven. The bird's gleaming black feathers blended with the wearer's black hair.

I gasped, straining to keep my eyes on the stranger as Carter twirled me around in our slow rotation. When I faced that direction again, the stranger was gone.

I looked for him for the rest of the night. I never saw him.

A NOTE FROM THE AUTHOR

Thank you for reading *Ghost of a Whisper*! I hope you're enjoying being a part of Betty's world.

Will you please leave a review for this book? Reviews mean everything to indie authors like me, and they help other readers connect with authors they might enjoy.

Thank you so much for your support!

Beth

ACKNOWLEDGMENTS

I am grateful to my test readers Tabatha, Andy and Karen, who give both great feedback and constant encouragement. And, as usual, I am indebted to my mom Ann for her editing.

NEXT IN THE SERIES

GHOST OF A MEMORY

BETTY BOO, GHOST HUNTER BOOK THREE

THE DEAD WALK AMONG THE LIVING IN GEORGIA.

A month after losing Maxwell, Betty "Boo" Boorman is feeling lonely, isolated, and desperate to get away from reminders of her demon ex-boyfriend. When rival ghost hunter Carter Lansford approaches Betty with a wild story about zombies, Betty jumps at the chance to investigate.

An abandoned island resort off the coast of Georgia is infested with the walking dead, and a preservation team has asked Betty and Carter for help. The only thing worse than spending two weeks on an uninhabited island with Carter is having the whole thing filmed for a new reality show.

As Betty tries to put on a brave face for the camera, she faces stubborn ghosts, rotting corpses, and one very handsome historian.

BOOKS BY BETH DOLGNER

The Betty Boo, Ghost Hunter Series

Paranormal Romance

Ghost of a Threat

Ghost of a Whisper

Ghost of a Memory

Ghost of a Hope

The Eternal Rest Bed and Breakfast Series

Paranormal Cozy Mystery

Sweet Dreams

Late Checkout

Picture Perfect

Scenic Views

Breakfast Included

Groups Welcome

Quiet Nights

The Nightmare, Arizona Series

Paranormal Cozy Mystery

Homicide at the Haunted House

Drowning at the Diner

Slaying at the Saloon

Murder at the Motel

Poisoning at the Party

Clawing at the Corral

Manifest

Young Adult Steampunk

A Talent for Death

Young Adult Urban Fantasy

Nonfiction

Georgia Spirits and Specters

Everyday Voodoo

ABOUT THE AUTHOR

Beth Dolgner writes paranormal fiction and nonfiction. Her interest in things that go bump in the night really took off on a trip to Savannah, Georgia, so it's fitting that her first series—Betty Boo, Ghost Hunter—takes place in that spooky city. Beth also writes paranormal nonfiction, including her first book, *Georgia Spirits and Specters*, which is a collection of Georgia ghost stories.

Beth and her husband, Ed, live in Tucson, Arizona. Their Victorian bungalow is possibly haunted, but it's not nearly as exciting as the ghostly activity at Eternal Rest Bed and Breakfast.

Beth also enjoys giving presentations on Victorian death and mourning traditions as well as Victorian Spiritualism. She has been a volunteer at an historic cemetery, a ghost tour guide, and a paranormal investigator. Beth likes to think of it all as research for her books.

Keep up with Beth and sign up for her newsletter at
BethDolgner.com.